# NIGHT TERRORS

## EDITED BY KAREN HENDERSON

KAYELLE PRESS

AUSTRALIA

First published in Australia in 2012

"A Ghost Story" by Mark Twain first published in 1870
"The Dead Girl" by Guy de Maupassant first published in 1887
"The Tell-Tale Heart" by Edgar Allan Poe first published in 1843

Kayelle Press, Australia
Email: admin@kayellepress.com
Website: www.kayellepress.com

National Library of Australia Cataloguing-in-Publication entry:
Night Terrors Anthology / edited by Karen Henderson
Short stories
Henderson, Karen, 1961–
ISBN 978-0-9808642-8-1
808.831

Cover artwork by Ken Henson
Text design by Kayelle Press

# CONTENTS

# A WORLD NOT OUR OWN

JC HEMPHILL

Tim heard on the news that the lines at the Conversion Centres were huge, but he wasn't expecting the horde of posers he and his buddy Davis found loitering around the entrance when they arrived. Women made up the majority of the converts waiting for, what they whole-heartedly believed was, their destiny. Tim could tell just by glancing at the elaborate costumes — hooded capes, plastic fangs, glittered skin, fake blood — and the unholy grins of adult-sized children that these people weren't like him. Their motivation for joining the colder side of living wasn't the same as his. These people had romanticised visions of what it was to be a vampire. They thought spending eternity in exile from the sun was about cheating death, indulgence, and lifetime-spanning love affairs.

But not Tim.

He wasn't volunteering for conversion because he thought being a vamp was 'hot'. He was doing it to find Jessie, his sister. She needed him. Their folks died when Tim was in college and Jessie was in high school. A tragic story, to be sure, but irrelevant. When they died, she moved in with Tim and his roommate in their college apartment. Tim dropped out so she could finish high school, became her provider, got her set up in her own place when she graduated, not too far from his apartment, and let her join the world.

Unfortunately, Jessie found acceptance of their parents' death in the macabre world of vampirism. She started dressing like them, acting like them, sleeping like them. She even had her incisors cosmetically lengthened to resemble fangs.

Then the suck-heads gained equal rights. And since it was their constitutional right to exist, it wasn't illegal to become one. Which meant they were free to recruit. Conversion Centres opened, inviting all humans to become Aeonian.

The suck-heads didn't call themselves vampires. They were smarter than that. The word 'vampire' exuded negativity. Two hundred years of literature and movies attached certain preclusions to the name, so they convinced the world that they were *Aeonians*. A shrewd marketing move, indeed. Aeonians made them sound like citizens of some country near Greece, nothing more fearful than the word 'Italian'.

Jessie, of course, lined up right away. That was two months ago. Nobody had seen her since, but her memory lingered with Tim like the scent of smoke in winter.

Davis parked the car in a garage down the street from the Centre and they walked. The Conversion Centre turned out to be more of a compound. Or maybe castle was a better word. Immense grey walls towered overhead, casting long shadows on the surrounding buildings. Tinted guard towers stood atop those walls at twenty-foot intervals, gleaming in the sun. A modern-gothic keep protruded several stories above the defensive perimeter.

Tim almost felt as if they were stepping into some giant asylum built for a world gone mad.

And maybe they were. Maybe they all were. Maybe they delivered themselves in groups of twos and threes to the greatest, longest madness of all.

"You sure you wanna go through with this, Tim?" Davis asked as they approached the compound. "I mean, I know I do, but you can still back out."

Davis was one of the vamp enthusiasts who thought converting would make life better. When the centres opened, Davis had burst into his apartment without knocking and waved a pamphlet on conversion in his face. Davis' eyes had glinted with the excitement of a child then.

But now, as they funnelled through goliath walls into a darkening compound crawling with vampires, his eyes didn't glint. He didn't even seem excited.

"I'm positive," said Tim. "You're the one with your tail tucked."

He hadn't told Davis about Jessie. In fact, he hadn't *really* told anyone. He'd heard the rumours about how the Aeonians gained equal rights in congress. And if it was even half true, then nobody would be able to help — not the police, not Homeland Security, not the Marines, not even your local congressman.

As for the media, they were nothing more than hype-men for the suck-heads.

Davis stood on his toes for a better view. Tim wondered if he could see anything over the bobbing heads and the thickening gloom. The Conversion Centre seemed to eclipse the entire sky. Only two windows interrupted the blank front of the building, both covered by steel shutters. He imagined them standing open at night, flames dancing within, transforming the daunting structure into a mouthless beast. The building — which was a living creature in his mind — didn't need a mouth. Not when streams of food marched willingly into its belly.

A twitch of anxiety rose. He pushed it away, reminding himself that this was the last place Jessie went before disappearing.

"Look," said Davis, pointing into the crowd.

"What?"

"Two of them are standing by the doors up ahead. I guess the walls block enough light for them to be outside."

Tim knew by 'them' he meant vampires. Despite the fact that they had their equality and were protected by the same laws we were, seeing a vamp was a rare thing. Not that they were hard to spot. Their pale skin and emaciated bodies made them walking spotlights in public.

"You ever wonder about these places?" said Tim. The crowd started to thicken and slow.

"How's that?" Davis asked absently.

"If so many people are converting, then why don't we see more suck-heads walking around? You know? They've got one of these centres in every major city and even some in not-so-major ones, and people are pumping into them around the clock, right?"

"I guess. Sounds like something Dirty Jenkins used to say. You remember him, right? That guy was out there. I wonder how long it takes once we're in the building."

"Dirty Jenkins might've been on to something. Look around. They let one of these groups in every hour, on the hour. Since we passed through those huge gates back there, how many people do you think we've seen? Couple hundred, right?" He didn't wait for an answer. "So multiply the amount of people there are here, by however many hours this place has been open. Then multiply that by how

8

many centres they have across the country. We should be seeing a vamp on every corner by now."

Davis shook his head. "What about the centres in Atlanta and Salt Lake? The news said almost nobody is going to those."

"Okay, but that's only two out of ... what? Thirty-five? Forty?"

"Forty-two."

"Okay. Forty-two. So where are they all?"

"The Aeonians?"

"Yeah," Tim almost yelled. "Where are all the damned vampires?"

"They only come out at night."

He almost countered, but decided not to. It wasn't like Davis would have an answer, anyways. They took small steps forward, shuffling in a tightening crowd. The two vamps Davis mentioned came into sight. One flanked each side of the double doors, both wearing the typical deadpan expression of the vampire.

He assumed the two vamps were ushers, there to keep people from trampling one another as they entered. But as they drew nearer, a low thrum radiated from within the building, and beyond the double doors he spotted a thick nest of shadows.

His heart seized, and an anxious thought crept into his mind. What if the two vamps weren't there to keep the peace? Maybe it was paranoia, but something told him, beyond all doubt, that their purpose was to ensure that those who went in did not come out.

He tried to dismiss the idea, but the thought of so many conversions without the streets being packed with vamps nagged like a persistent itch. Was there an exit on the other side of the building where these streams of people — now vampires — exited after the process was over? Did they go home and get in bed with their human spouses and return to work? No, of course not. They couldn't survive in sunlight. Then where did they go? And why wasn't the news talking about *that* instead of how long the lines are?

Tim suddenly wanted to run, and from the looks of him, Davis did too. Only the surging crowd behind kept Davis from fleeing.

The thrumming grew louder and, for a moment, seemed to match the beating of Tim's heart.

He wondered if Jessie had been scared at this point or if she was like all the other wannabes here. Glancing around, he could almost see anticipation wafting from the crowd. They smiled and laughed and pretended to bite each other's necks. The menacing tower before them went unnoticed. Like people waiting to enter a haunted house who are enthralled by the chainsaw in the background, the thrumming — which had mutated into a grinding, gear-driven heart — was a mere soundtrack for the adventure to come.

Tim and Davis crammed through the double-doors into a narrow hallway, following a set of chattering women. Behind them was a family of six who clasped hands in a desperate attempt to stick together. After twenty feet, the hall opened into a torch lit foyer with a balcony overlooking the incoming crowd.

Davis pulled Tim toward the outer wall, letting the family behind move on. "Truth be told," he whispered. "I don't think I can go through with this. I mean, you made a good point earlier. Where are all the vampires? And this place. It isn't right. I don't know what, but something is wrong here."

Tim noticed he dropped 'Aeonians' for 'vampires', and a

part of him wished he could smile. "Yeah, well ... truth be told, I'm not here because I want to transition."

Davis' eyebrows lifted, and then dropped back to their neutral position. "I figured."

"You did?"

"Yeah, Tim. I did." Davis glanced around. Two vamps stood on the balcony, but their eyes remained fixed on the line of people as they continued deeper into the building. The converts split into four separate tunnels, each with a sign reading 'Meet Your Maker — This Way'. Tim was reminded of the ads they had on TV about conversion. The vamps made the process sound as painless and carefree as going to the movies. They used cute terms like 'conversion' and 'joining eternity' as ways to soften the blow of what really went on behind the grey walls of their centres. 'Meet Your Maker' was the Disney version of saying 'Hey lambs, this way to your slaughter'.

Davis' eyes softened as he continued. "I've known you for a long time. A long long time. So I know you're worried about Jess. You try to hide it, but I know you too well. And what you said about the vampires is true. You haven't seen her since she went in, have you?"

He couldn't speak, so he shook his head. Here he was, thinking he was slick and cool and calm about the whole thing, and Davis knew all along. He felt foolish, but Davis' question soon brought Tim back to the real shame roiling in his mind — Jessie — and then all he felt was fear. His chest heaved in a kind of bodily hiccup as he fought the urge to cry.

"You're here to find her, huh?"

"Yes," Tim replied in a choked voice. He cleared his throat, met Davis' eyes, and said with added conviction, "Yes."

Davis stepped back, and shook his head as if he were very displeased. "All right. I'll keep going with you then."

"Before you commit, you outta know something. I've heard things. Like why we haven't seen Dirty Jenkins in a while. Like how our government has covered this all up because these parasites have burrowed so deep into our—"

A woman cried out as she stumbled out of line. Two of her friends tried to help her up, but she recoiled, scooting backwards on the marble floor. Tears streaked her face.

"NO," she screamed at her friends. "I *won't* go in. I don't want to do this anymore."

Her friends pleaded with her to stand up, but she refused. She changed her mind; she didn't want to be Aeonian anymore; she wanted to leave. She scrambled to her feet and started back toward the hall they came from. Before she took more than three steps, metal doors slammed closed, severing her and Tim and Davis and everyone else from the incoming flow. Muffled cries of confusion came from the hall side, and those left in the foyer stopped and watched as the woman threw her body against the doors. They held firm and sent her tumbling back.

The two vamps on the balcony vanished and seemed to materialise next to the woman.

"Something tells me we don't have a choice anymore," Tim whispered.

The woman looked from one bony figure to the other and started screaming. Each vamp grabbed a wrist, sneered, and then all three blurred for an instant and disappeared.

The few who witnessed the abduction gasped, and as some began to understand — as the harsh facts seeped into their brains and the beautiful veil hiding the grotesque face of vampirism was lifted — shouts and panicked utterances spread around the room.

Tim ran to the spot where the woman had been. Standing there somehow confirmed her absence, and people started rushing toward the door. They banged, clawed, and pled to be released. They were desperate. The horrors in the haunted house were real and more deadly than advertised. Tim somehow found time to wonder if any of them would use the term Aeonian now or if they would fall back to the old standard as Davis had. He wanted to scream at them 'what the hell did you think you were going to find? These are VAMPIRES. They are. Call them what you want, but they are — in the most gruesome, bloodsucking, human and soul devouring way — VAMPIRES.'

Davis grabbed Tim's shoulder and pointed at the balcony. Tim's breath froze. What he saw filled his bones with an aching terror. Ten of the tallest, leanest vampires he had ever seen lined the balcony. They were so perfect and white that they could've passed for clothed statues. Others noticed and turned to face the new fear. Despair and panic in the room doubled.

Voices smoothed by eons of use issued from all ten vampires in unison. "Continue forward."

Two young men started running on command, each disappearing down a different tunnel. The rest cowered, unsure of what to do next. Their bodies and minds begged them to escape, to get the hell away from this place by any means possible. But the inevitability of the situation made the vampires impossible to disobey. A few people seemed to think they still had a choice in the matter, but they were fooling themselves.

The only real choice any of them had was: Do I want to

walk *or* do I want to be dragged down one of those tunnels?

"Continue forward," the voices commanded, and the ten vampires on the level above were suddenly among the crowd. Tim didn't even see them move. They were on the balcony, then the ground.

A woman screamed, but her husband covered her mouth and urged her toward the tunnels. Others did as they were told, and soon Tim and Davis were moving as well. Most chose the same path. Probably because they hoped to find safety in numbers.

Tim sensed the vamps behind them, watching to ensure they didn't retreat. He almost turned to look, but forced himself not to. He would play the good-little-lamb.

As they progressed, the tunnel graded into new depths of darkness. The walls shook as the thrumming-grinding sound from earlier returned. It reverberated from somewhere ahead, and he was reminded of how the building had looked like a sleeping monster with steel shutters pulled over its eyes and a thrumming, mechanical heart.

The darkness blanketed the others and sank Tim into an abysmal sense of solitude.

"Davis?" he said, and almost jumped at his own voice. The sound of shuffling feet was the only response. He moved onward, touching the wall every few steps to keep his bearings.

"Davis," he tried again. Only feet scuffing the stone floor. "Anybody?"

Someone mumbled, but they sounded distant. The hall seemed to distort space and sound because he shouldn't have been more than a few feet from a dozen other people.

The thrumming added pressure to the situation. He

almost couldn't take it. It was so overpowering and horrid in the way it grew and shrank in intensity — ranging from heavy whomps like a room full of subwoofers, to the screeching of metal working against metal — that he couldn't concentrate. His thoughts came in fragments, provoking his sanity.

He pictured Jessie walking down the same hallway, hearing the same ominous heartbeat. He pictured vampires swarming over her in the dark, eating and tearing at her flesh while she screamed for the pain to end. Jessie was replaced by memories of all the people making their way through the Conversion Centre, unaware of what waited. They had no idea. Because really, *he* still had no idea of what lay ahead.

He bumped into something solid. He reached out and felt a cold stone wall. To his right was a gleaming speck of light. It was orange and weak, but it glimmered in the dark with all the magnificence of the sun.

He jogged toward it. The light began illuminating the walls, and he noticed several off-shoots that split the tunnel into divergent paths, none of which had a light at the end. He had probably lost Davis and the group to one or several of these off-shoots.

The light flickered — torches.

Inching toward the new room, he peered around the corner. The original group — that misguided horde of wannabes dressed like their favourite suck-heads — waited in a tight pack. They stood with their backs turned, watching a screen with the words 'Meet Your Maker' displayed in large crimson letters.

To his horror, the atmosphere was still light and excited.

These people had no idea. They hadn't seen the woman break down. They hadn't seen her ripped away against her will.

The scene overwhelmed him. "RUN. THEY TOOK A WOMAN WHO WANTED TO LEAVE. THEY JUST TOOK HER. AND I THINK THEY KILLED HER."

A field of confused faces looked back. Some scrunched their eyebrows in worry, others whispered to a neighbour.

An obese man stepped forward. "Ain't that why we're here? To get killed?"

Several people chuckled at the comment, followed by a torrent of laughter.

Then the lights went out. A gaunt man with a very proper air about him replaced the words on the screen, and the room turned its attention toward the change.

"Hello," the man on the screen said. His voice was soothing and rich, almost hypnotic. "Welcome to Conversion. Are you ready to meet your maker?" His lips pulled back in a tight-lipped grin, revealing the tips of his fangs.

The crowd responded with claps, cheers, and whoops. Tim remained stupefied.

"Splendid," the man said. "Let me begin by thanking you for coming. We are pleased that you elected to join the Aeonian lifestyle." Someone in the crowd whistled their approval. "My name is Sven, and I've been an Aeonian for over one hundred years. I understand some of you may be nervous. Don't be. I can tell you that I do miss my mortal life at times, but only in a nostalgic manner — as when adults say they wish they could return to the innocence of youth. And now, you volunteers *may* have the opportunity to live as I have lived."

Sven grinned again. Despite the fangs, the slight emotion in his face was somehow disarming. It made Tim want to trust him and his lullaby words.

"*But*," Sven began. A quick memory came to mind: Jessie, years ago when their parents were still around, telling Tim 'only shit and farts follow a *but*.' "I've got some good news and I've got some bad news." The grin didn't waver. A murmur spread around the room, but nothing more than mild curiosity. "You humans eat desert last because it tastes the best and because that is the flavour you wish to leave the meal with. And for this same reason, I prefer getting the nasty news out of the way first. Keeps me from leaving with a bad taste in my mouth."

Someone shouted agreement. Probably the same rowdy convert who had whistled.

Tim wanted to yell out — people should be running, not listening to Sven — but he couldn't. He couldn't do anything. He was rooted in place just like all the others. He wanted to move, but his legs and the ground were as one, and moving his legs would require moving the ground and everything it was attached to.

"Okay, the bad news, as promised. When you entered the foyer of this building, you entered the conversion process. The process contains two parts — Conversion and Sustainability. And, well, only one of four tunnels led to eternal life among the Aeonians. But," *only shit and farts follow a but*, "the other three led to Sustainability. We'll get to that in a moment."

The general consensus of the crowd was confusion. They heard the words, but didn't quite comprehend them. The slow drawing of conclusions surfaced on some faces faster than others. Before real surprise could set in, Sven continued.

"Now, the good news, and I say this with great pleasure," hope rose collectively in the room, "you fine folks, did *not* take the tunnel to eternity. You *will*, however, be meeting your maker today ... just not the one you thought it would be." He grinned and all the disarming qualities dissipated, replaced by a cruel sneer that hinted of perverse joy. "If you listen closely, you can hear the grinders deep beneath the building. That's our little disposal system. You're bloodless bodies will feed it soon." Sven paused, savouring the tension. "I never said the news was good for *you*, now did I? Welcome to Sustainability."

The screen went black, plunging the room into a lightless void.

Tim's heart burst when the screams began. He sensed movement. A stampede of feet pattered against the ground, followed by crashing sounds he assumed were people tripping and being trampled in the ensuing chaos. Slower shapes of humans grazed him as people blindly swarmed in the darkness. Colder shapes, mere wisps of air, followed the slower ones, picking through them with viscous speed.

The terrorised cries became a single crescendo of fear. Ripping, falling, ravaging sounds pierced the screams. Tim turned, searched for the tunnels, searched for anything to grasp, searched for anything to save him, but found nothing.

He pressed against a wall, trying in vain to see through the blackness. A woman ran screaming, head-first, into the wall near him. She crumpled to the ground, sobbing. Then the sobbing was gone, replaced by a wet sucking. He couldn't see it, but the vampire's presence was unmistakable.

He wondered how Jessie reacted to all this. She must've been terrified beyond words. So young and fragile, she probably felt helpless. Lost.

He did.

He suddenly picked up on the thrumming-grinding heart — the human disposal. It was there all along, but he had somehow forgotten about it. Time seemed to alter speeds with the sound, ramping up on the grinding parts and slowing to a lethargic crawl when it changed to a low thrum. He pictured someone dropping chunks of meat into a blender — loud and screaming while empty, but slowing and altering pitch as flesh bogs the motor down.

Thin fingers slipped around his forearm. He tried to pull away, but the grip clamped, shackling him in place. It pulled him closer, yanking him toward the torso on the other end. Bones pressed against his, embracing him, holding him like a child's doll. The metallic scent of blood made him gag. The vampire pressed its face against his, spreading heat through him, and for a moment, he thought maybe it wasn't a vampire at all. Vampires aren't warm. They're the temperature of death.

But it wasn't inner-warmth. It was the blood of the woman next to him.

He tried to squirm away, but the embrace only constricted, crushing flesh into viscera. He shuddered, giving in beneath the power. The vampire blew a feminine stream of air over his ear, mocking his fear, reminding him that this was but a game.

Tim shut his eyes and awaited the bite to come.

Soon, the sting of a predator's fangs would pierce his neck and his blood would license some suck-head to continue living forever, killing, spreading the greatest, longest madness of all.

"I've missed you," the vampire whispered. It sounded just like Jessie. He recognized the funny way she dragged her S's out. At long last, he found her. "I've missed you dearly, brother. *But...*"

# Night Terrors

# CORRIDORS

## CAROLE HALL

3 a.m. The Death Hour. Carl Roberts jerked awake at the ringing of the phone. It was the business land-line not his mobile phone.

"Who in blazes is calling at this hour?" he said out loud in the dark room. He was in the concrete business, laying it, and nobody in their right mind would want to know about concrete in the middle of the night.

"Hello?" he croaked through sleep laden vocal cords, grabbing up the receiver like it was something dirty. A bright moon was laying silver stripes across the far wall.

"Hello?" he said again, louder, holding the phone closer to his ear.

"Who is it?" There was a hollow, empty sound vibrating down the phone line. Like the wind blowing down a long tunnel, yet he felt someone on the other end.

"It's Nao..." then the line went dead.

"What?" he said, before realising, then dropped the white phone back onto its cradle. Outside the wind had picked up. The long leaves of the mimosa tree rattled against his bedroom window and he shivered.

The phone suddenly rang again. He jumped so hard his

heart missed a beat. "What the hell?" he gasped out loud, grabbing the phone, meaning to give the caller a piece of his mind.

"Who are you and what do you want? It's three o'clock in the damn morning!" He was steaming mad now.

"It's Naomi," said a woman's voice so far away it quivered and broke into pieces. "Naomi." The line went dead again.

Carl felt the blood drain from his face so fast he thought he might faint. Can't be. He swallowed, blinked and wondered if he was dreaming. Yet he touched his hands and felt the coolness of his flesh. He was awake. God, he was *so* awake and listening to someone telling him *what*?

The only Naomi he knew was dead. Years ago. A suicide. In her car.

He had been just twenty-three and so in love with this fine girl with her long auburn hair, her dimpled cheek and smile that broke his heart. Naomi. But she had loved Jack. Not him. Never him. Carl Roberts might have been an insect for all the notice Naomi took. It was always Jack. Tall, blonde, broad-shouldered Jack. Blue-eyed, very married Jack. With six very Jack kids. Didn't matter, Carl Roberts loved this woman so many years ago that he never let a day go by that he didn't think about Naomi. Was that true unrequited love? Betcha.

He was ready when the phone jangled its eerie call a third time.

"What do you want?" he asked in a voice so cool, throwing his legs over the side of the bed. "Who in blazes are you?"

He heard again the whistling sound, the long tunnel, like at the end of the world phone call, here in his bedroom at the death hour.

"It's Naomi," said the voice. He closed his eyes. Get a grip.

"Can't be. You're dead."

"I know."

Right. That's established. Whoever this fool was knew he had her number.

So to speak.

The gruff bark of a neighbour's dog filtered through the open window.

"It is me. Naomi. I'm here in the corridors."

Now he was taken off balance, for a second. The phone in his hand trembled. "Explain."

"It's hard."

"You think it's hard for you. News flash, you're dead, long gone, some joker who's playing a joke at three a.m. and you say it's hard. Either talk, tell me what you want or shut up and go away. That plain enough?"

"Carl, please."

He breathed so deeply he thought his lungs might overload. She knew his name! He gripped the phone as if it was a life-line. Perhaps it was.

He heard the wind playing against the window pane again, eager to be reaching in only stopped by solid glass. For now. He waited.

"When I died I came to another plain," it really was her voice. A relative? No, it was Naomi and he was going mad. Did insane people know they were crazy?

"Like a long corridor with doors on either side, but they don't open, I've tried. But I can see you."

The whistling intensified down the line. He was actually standing now, leaning against the east wall for support, his pyjamas slipping down his legs. He jerked them up with his left hand.

"Naomi, if you are who you say you are, answer me one question and then we can talk," he planned to catch this imposter dead to rights.

"I know all about you, Carl."

Softer now, as if smiling, patient.

He took the initiative.

"Fine, listen up. You and I danced only once. What colour was your dress and where were we?"

Now I've gotcha.

He recalled the feel of her in his arms. She was so tanned and smelled of sea and sand and a French perfume that he would never ever forget when he smelled it years later on other women, although there had never, ever, been another woman who wore it like Naomi. It had been a night filled with silver stars at the Arawak hotel and her gown had been blue chiffon. He waited. This was it.

And then the voice on the phone told him. Everything, date, time and place and no one else could have known such details.

Sweat popped out on his forehead. It was Naomi and he was talking to the dead. Get outta here!

"Carl?"

"What?"

"You were in love with me but I only wanted Jack."

Oh, yes, he remembered Jack all right. You got that right. A ladies man down to the holes in the knees of his jeans. A New Yorker. A heart crusher. And he used her and left her and she killed herself on a March day filled with rain. In a parking lot with a hose through the window of her blue Buick Skylark.

"Carl, it's lonely here, but I can tell you something no one else living knows, if you're interested." How did a land-line suddenly become so extraordinarily useful?

"Hey, I'm awake, so knock yourself out," he told her nonchalantly, sitting back on the edge of his bed, his feet straight out in front.

He heard her voice again, low now, trying to sincerely convince him it was her.

"When you die by your own hand, as I did, you are in the corridors. That's the best way I can describe this place. Then something good happens and you can open a door and wait to move on to another level. There are nine of them, each higher and purer than the one you leave behind. And the ninth is Nirvana and Age of Enlightenment and you are free to choose to come back or stay. But only love can..."

Her voice crackled, began to fade, then came back.

"You there?"

Where else would he be, he thought. This is madness.

"What do you have to do to move up?" he asked. Let's get this show on the road. This was one hell of a dream.

"Wait, let me tell you more about this place, okay?"

He shrugged, the clock at his bedside table read 3:12 a.m. "Your dime," he said, then smiled at the absurdity of his remark.

"Everything is known here, what will happen in the future is a given. I can tell you when earthquakes will occur, when nations will change hands, when monarchs will be born and die, when the Messiah will eventually arrive back because there is, my friend, *there really is a God of all mankind*, if that makes you feel any better."

Strangely it did. He had lost faith these long years. Not knowing, so much trouble on this planet, why would a loving — well, never mind all that.

"Great," he said shaking his head, trying to correlate what this voice from the dead or whatever was laying on him like so much peanut butter and jam.

"If I believe anything you've said, give me the Super Lotto numbers for this week and I'll be as happy as a lark. Never mind the after-life, let's make this one a humdinger, okay?" His short burst of laughter echoed in the darkness.

The phone went dead. He stared at it in frank surprise. "Hello?"

Then he shook it angrily. "Hello? Hello?" What the?

He literally spent the rest of the daylight hours waiting for the phone to ring. It did. With orders. Mrs. Harvey wanted a concrete slab for her jacuzzi, the Donaldson's were building an addition to the beach-house property and needed concrete work, Bill King wanted a new patio for his grill. All of them he put off, saying he was full up, right now.

He put on clean pyjamas and climbed into bed a little after ten p.m. Not to sleep, to wait. For the death hour. Because he was almost, not quite, but *almost* certain the phone would ring. He'd thought about pulling the plug, disconnecting the thing. He had his mobile phone and after all it was night-time. But he didn't do anything but lie in his clean bed and wait for the phone to ring. And try to figure it out.

It had begun to rain earlier in the day. Clouds moved in across a steel gray sky. Autumn had given way to the first cold fingers of winter and the rain that splashed against the roof and his window panes had a hard insistent, bullying feel to it.

"Come on," he whispered. "Come on." He heard the clock ticking.

Death hour.

Three sixteen a.m.

Three nineteen.

He jumped when the phone sprang to life at three twenty-one a.m.

"Carl?" Do you believe me now?" said Naomi's voice and he closed his eyes as tears formed and escaped.

"Yes. What do you want, Naomi?" he spoke her name for the first time.

"I want you to love me again," she said.

"I never stopped," he answered her. "Never in all the years."

"You have to prove it." Her voice was soft and low like a leaf leaving a tree and floating earthwards.

"How can I prove something so abstract to a dead person?' he hated saying that as he gripped the phone. "It doesn't even matter any more," he felt compelled to hang on to some semblance of reality.

"Yes, it does. I can show you the way," she offered. "Would you like to turn back the clock and be with me always, as if Jack never happened?"

The rain began a crescendo of sound and fury, battering, hammering the house.

"You can do that?" he asked, his voice beginning to tremble. "How?"

"Only once," Naomi's voice answered. "You can come to me if you truly love me. I have the key to opening the door to this plain and I can let you in, but I can only use the key once. Do you understand?"

He listened to every word she said, shaking his head from side to side like a dog trying to get the water free from his coat.

"I haven't a clue what you're talking about. How can I understand a voice from the dead on my telephone unless one of us is plain, fucking nuts?" Now he was irritated, still curious though. "What are you talking about?"

"Think about it, Carl," she said as the phone went dead again.

And so he did, think about being with Naomi again, without Jack ever having been in the picture. Could she turn back time? Nah. No one could do that. Then what? Was he losing his mind during the Death Hour when the phone kept ringing and the woman he had loved all those years ago, who had surely died, had he not received an obituary in the mail from her sister? And had he not wept?

Three eighteen a.m. He was ready. By God he was ready. No rain this night, just the silver moon again sliding across lovely soft clouds.

"Carl?"

The same low, husky voice like the remnants of a cold.

Carl pounced in, quick-like, without so much as a hello-how-are-you?

"You said you have the key to wherever you are; some plain just above earth I gather, but I need to know more about this astral, phenomenal sphere, netherland, outerland, that no one but you knows about. Real time, now, Naomi, did you really kill yourself or just run away and hide for all these years and you're alive in some backwoods place, huh? Did Jacky-boy give you the heave-ho and you disappeared into a nunnery and now you escaped? For the life of me I can't make heads or tails of these night time calls, so come straight and lay it all out, because this is positively the last time I'm going to talk to you unless you level with me, capice?"

He heard the almost human in-take of breath through the phone.

"Carl, it is as I said, I am in the corridors, the lower level of this plain. If someone loves me enough to join me I can move up to the next corridor which is number eight. We

28

can be together, don't you understand? This is not life as you know it, there are many different kinds of life on different planets we know nothing about. You think earth is the only place to sustain life? There are hundreds beyond the strongest telescope invented, but incredibly there waiting to be discovered. Millions of light years from earth, life everlasting."

"Wait, are you saying if I give up this life, I get another, with you, for all time?" he asked, flushing, the idea broadening in his mind. Wow.

"Exactly, my dear Carl. I can make it easy for you. Remember the Valium you got from the doctor when you had trouble sleeping?"

"Uh, huh," he answered. In the medicine cabinet, blue pills, ten mg's.

"And the bottle of Vodka you got last Christmas?"

How on earth did she know all this? Right on the money.

"One last question, Carl. Are you in love or close to anyone back there?"

Back there? Oh, here. He thought about that. No. All he did was work, have a couple of beers with the guys sometimes after work, watch a Sunday football game, but there wasn't anyone. Mary had passed away years back. He got married because it was the thing to do, then. Now that he had time to think about it, yes, he was lonely, just going through months and years until old age stopped his heart and the earthen grave got his bones.

"Then what?" he asked, knowing she'd figured it all out. He could almost see her smile. That beautiful, wide, heartbreaking smile that he'd never seen again on any other female. Oh, how he ached to see it again. And it made up his mind.

"Okay."

"Just come to me. It's all up to you now."

The rain stopped sometime during the next night. The leaves of his mimosa tree hung with the wetness he didn't see. Closing down the business, cutting off the water and electricity, no pets to take care off, smiling to himself, thinking of what was to come. At last, being with his love: Naomi.

Sitting in his cosy overstuffed armchair, duly shaved, hair combed, clean shirt and pants. He'd slowly emptied the bottle of Valium and drunk the full bottle of vodka until he just left his life behind forever at three-fourteen a.m.

"Hello," she said, holding out her arms in greeting as he stepped into her corridor. He looked around. It was a long, very long dark place with many doors on either side. He was here, with her, at last.

"Now what?" he asked smiling, moving toward her.

"Now, goodbye," she said, as the door behind her opened, she stepped in and bright light shone through, blinding him.

Then the door closed tight and he couldn't for the life of him open it.

# Death Crone

## Jonathan Shipley

The sibilant whispers floated up from the temple crypt like snakes on the wind. "Sssister ... do not desert usss ... Saraid our ssister."

The Death Crone dozing before the fire in the chamber above stirred at the sound of her name and turned to scowl at the open archway behind her. Desert them? How could she? Her future was ordained. She shuddered at the prospect of being laid in that same crypt to moulder and whisper to her successor until her own rotting body crumbled to dust. The price of necromancy was great. Those who stole death's secrets forfeited its release.

But these were not idle whispers. The dead were uneasy and that bespoke dire happenings in the world beyond the temple walls. All happenings were dire these days, it seemed. But news would come soon enough. It always did. Saraid huddled closer to the fire, cursing the ache in her bones.

A hesitant knock sounded at her door. "Old Mother, will you come out?" a husky voice called from the corridor.

Saraid frowned as she pulled herself out of her high-backed chair. She recognised the voice and found it unseemly that the head of the temple should come knocking in the night like an acolyte. In her younger days, Saraid had ruled with much more dignity. Her successors were weak. All of these latter-day priestesses were weak.

"Old Mother, there is another messenger from the lowlands," said the High Matron as Saraid opened the door. "We need your wisdom in our councils."

Saraid nodded, noting with a crooked smile how quickly the Matron retreated down the corridor. When she had been High Matron, Saraid had also feared this room over the crypts. She, however, had been clever enough to send others as messengers.

As she approached the Common Room, the smell of wood smoke told her that the central fire pit had been stoked high where usually it would be banked for the night. She paused at the doorway to straighten as best she could, and then stepped into the flickering light of the flames. The gathering was large for that hour of the night. Even a few of the younger priestesses were in attendance, looking as sombre as their elders. Did they already know the news from the lowlands? Of course, they did, thought Saraid. They would have discussed the news at length and only brought her into the council when all other possibilities were exhausted.

"A messenger came from the temple at Rhiordan," said the High Matron, wringing her hands nervously. "Soldiers burned it to the ground with the sisters inside."

"Lowlanders or Northmen?" asked Saraid.

The matron shrugged. "Is there any difference these days? The barbarians have tainted all the lowland clans. The island kingdoms are falling and the cursed dragon-warriors are slaughtering all who render homage to the Old Way."

"Or perhaps this is what they believe due homage is," cackled Saraid. "A splendid pyre with burnt offerings." The others shifted uncomfortably at the joke. "That was the last of the lowland temples, was it not?" she asked.

The High Matron nodded. "The Stone Circles still stand, but we are the only true temple left in all the islands. What should we do?"

"Death is on the march," answered Saraid. "There is little we can do. The destruction at Rhiordan is only one more link in the chain of death."

"Consult the crypts, Old Mother," begged another priestess. "We need the guidance of our undying sisters below."

Saraid nodded mechanically, but she felt a strange reluctance to descend into the crypts tonight. The talk of death had conjured up the image of her own future, and that was never pleasant.

From the Common Room, she crossed the courtyard and climbed the wall overlooking the road. The parapet was thick with crows, all huddled together in unnatural silence as they stared at her with bright eyes. Waiting. An omen, she realised immediately. But what was the meaning? Then a movement in the moonlight caught her attention. There below she saw a stranger staring up at her, a stranger shadowed by some darkness deeper than the night itself.

A voice sounded in her mind. *Come down, Old Mother. The end comes. Let us strike a bargain.*

Saraid hissed and drew back. The mindtouch left a stench that she recognised all too well. She did not strike bargains with undead creatures. The fact that a *dearg-dul*, a revenant, even dared approach her was galling. Once such creatures would have feared a Death Crone's power more than iron itself. She turned and sought her own chamber.

"The world is crumbling," she murmured to herself as she sat once again before the banked fire. "My world is crumbling." She remembered her promise at council and grimaced. The crypts felt alien and dangerous tonight.

From the arched stairway at her back, the whispers answered. "Ssister ... do not desert uss."

Saraid shifted uncomfortably. The autumn chill made her bones ache. How long had it been since she had been free of aches? Years? Decades? Would death at least take the ache away?

With a sigh she heaved herself to her feet, crossed to the archway, and descended to the crypts. She carried no torch for she had no desire to see the decaying forms whose guidance she sought. But there was no putting this off any longer.

"Answer me, my sisters," she called when she stood at the bottom of the steps. "What fate awaits the temple?"

A low moan issued forth from the alcoves, but nothing more.

"What fate awaits?" Saraid asked again, and this time the whispers floated toward her.

"Do not desert ussss..."

The plea became more insistent and behind it Saraid heard an unexpected scraping sound. The sound of bone on bone and bone on stone. There was movement in the alcoves where the corpses lay. She peered through the darkness and retreated a step towards the stairway as the crypt suddenly filled with hunger — hunger for something beyond their stone beds. She had never known the dead to be so active or so demanding. It was as if they were reaching out their dead limbs to take her among them.

Saraid fled up the stairs.

What do they know? she kept asking herself as she sought the fires of the central hall. The dead seemed more interested in her than in the future of the temple. The undead stranger's words came back to her, and suddenly she realised that was the connection. They knew what was about to unfold with the stranger, the *dearg-dul* — and feared it. She thought back. There had been something inexplicable about him — not just the arrogance, but the taste of something strangely familiar.

Saraid spent the next few days waiting and watching from the wall. What bargain would the stranger offer her? What would happen if she accepted? Old tales came back to her, tales of the dead rising in anger against the living. To betray the crypts was to invite the most perilous of curses.

Then another messenger of sorts arrived — a headless corpse tied to the saddle of a post horse. Weaklings, Saraid thought in contempt, as she watched panic spread throughout the temple. A strong leader could have controlled the confusion.

Saraid glanced down at her own withered arms. If her body had possessed the strength, Saraid would have seized control once more in the temple's hour of need. She longed for the power to make the Northmen pay for their desecration, even though it cost the life of every remaining priestess.

As Saraid turned, the High Matron came scurrying across the courtyard.

"Old Mother," puffed the woman. "I have been seeking

you everywhere. You must summon the dead to our defence."

The thought of releasing the dead filled Saraid with sudden apprehension. It had not been done in her lifetime, but the lore contained plentiful warnings. Once unleashed, the dead were not easy to bind to the crypt again. And there was always a price.

"It is no army that lies in the crypts," she answered hurriedly. "Half-rotted corpses are ill-suited to fight a pitched battle."

She saw that the Matron was unconvinced and added, "The lowland Death Crones would have tried that defence, and it did not save their temples." She walked quickly away.

Saraid paced the outer walls at dawn, watching the vanguard of the approaching troops snaking through the passes to the rocky uplands. The desire to smite them welled up within her like a burning hunger. Desecrators. Destroyers.

A slight movement distracted her gaze and she noticed the shadowed stranger waiting in the orchards beyond the wall. *Finally*, she thought. *Now to find out.*

*Come down*, his mind-voice urged. This time she descended to meet him.

He stood cloaked in grey and sable. "Be at peace, Old Mother," he said. "I mean you no harm."

"I do not fear you, *dearg-dul*," Saraid responded haughtily. "I am the Death Crone, the ultimate face of the Eternal." As she spoke, she called on the remnants of her power to lend her an aspect as dreadful as her title, but the stranger did not cower back.

"I am aware of your office," he answered with the hint of a smile.

Saraid felt both annoyance and unease as she let the illusion fade. "What do you want here, creature?" she snapped.

"I bring an offer — a chance to escape the coming butchery."

"Why?"

The stranger gave a soft chuckle. "The Dark Path, Old Mother. In life I was a seeker of knowledge. I still seek, but now nothing less than the secret of life and death will satisfy me. The Death Crones have the secret knowledge—"

Suddenly it became clear. "Do you really think I will waste the Dark Mother's mysteries of life and death on some petty undead sorcerer? There is no help for you here."

"Wait!" he commanded and Saraid could feel the power behind the word. But she was no novice. She cast off the compulsion and turned to go.

"The end comes swiftly, Old Mother," he added quickly. "The barbarians will be here within the hour."

Saraid cackled. "And yet you stand here bargaining. I think, creature, your plight must be as desperate as mine. Your search is a fool's quest. If my knowledge brought the kind of power you envision, I could strike down the Northmen and be done with them. And you." She started back toward the postern gate, but paused as the stranger gave a low laugh.

"There is power," he said, "and there is power. You and I together we could summon fire to blast the Northmen, but by myself I lack the knowledge to fully utilise what I possess. You have the knowledge that transcends death itself."

"Death is the only truth." Though Saraid replied automatically with the words from the litanies, her thoughts fastened on the stranger's claim. Did he truly have the power to blast the Northmen?

"No, there is more. There is this…" He threw back his cloak to reveal a heavy amulet about his neck with silver and copper intertwined to form a scrolled symbol. Then he quickly covered it again.

Saraid's eyes widened in recognition. The Rune of Earthfire. Her body trembled at the magnitude of that recognition. It was one of three set to guard the island kingdoms. The Earthfire should have been buried at the heart of the Great Circle on the southern plains, just as the Rune of Sea was buried within the Callanish Circle to the north, and the Wind Rune in a circle on the Western isle.

The threads of events were connected, it appeared. The southern plains were no longer protected and had been the first to fall to the Northmen. And now with the ancient Guard of Three disrupted, the other kingdoms were falling as well. So the lore warned would happen, and safeguards had been placed to avert this very doom. The first Death Crones had warded the Runes with Death herself that none disturb their resting places.

Her mouth quirked into a bitter rictus grin. All brought to naught by a revenant, immune from Death for he was already dead. He had dug up the Rune and doomed them all.

"There is much that I know," the *dearg-dul* continued, sensing nothing of her dismay. "But the manipulation of this amulet — for that I need your mysteries." He paused and glanced back down the road as a trumpet sounded in the distance. "They come. You are the last Death Crone in the island kingdoms. Do not throw your knowledge away."

Saraid looked to the bend in the road where the Northmen would shortly appear, and back to the *dearg-dul* — the joint murderers of the Old Way. Would that she could destroy all these desecrators.

"I can save your sisters," added the stranger more urgently. "This last stronghold of the Old Way can survive, even though the Old Way be forgotten in the rest of the land. The kingdoms are falling."

"Indeed they do fall." Saraid thought again of the reason for that, tasted again the cup of bitterness. A fluttering of wings drew her gaze to the branches above. The orchard was filled with silent, waiting crows. Waiting more patiently than the whispering dead. She gave a start. The whispers in the crypt had been right all long. They were telling her what was to be done.

"Give me the knowledge, and I can strike down the lead troops as they round the bend," offered the stranger.

"Perhaps that would be best," Saraid answered slowly. She must not appear too eager. "It is very old knowledge you seek, the oldest treasure of the temple. Its key lies in the most ancient alcove within the crypts." She paused, tensed. Would he sense the trap? Had this sorcerer gleaned enough to realise the danger of the crypts?"

An expression of smug satisfaction crept across his face. "Then we have accord. It seems, Old Mother, that we are not so unlike one another after all."

She bit back a response and led the way through the postern and through the corridors to her own chambers. Then down the stone steps to the dark doorway. All was quiet, unnaturally so. At no time in her years as Death Crone had the dead rested so easily. "This way," she said and stepped into the crypts.

The *dearg-dul* followed, conjuring pale werelight to light the way. He barely glanced at the half-rotted forms in the alcoves. The dead were of little interest to the undead, apparently. He did not see the silent stirrings within the alcoves as he passed by. Oh, they could be quiet when there was need. Saraid fought back the urge to giggle. The dead, the undead, and a Death Crone — what a dance they made.

The revenant reached the solid stone of the far wall. "Where is the alcove with its secret?" he demanded, turning. "What...?"

Saraid had already slipped away and was nearly at the steps when it began. He had strength and sorcery on his side, but there were so many of them crowding in upon him. And the dead were so hard to kill.

From the steps she watched the struggle until the werelight sputtered into darkness. Then she waited in the darkness. The sounds of limbs ripping whispered around her — their limbs, his limbs. A *dearg-dul* could not survive the severing of his head. The dead below would all know that.

When all was quiet, she again advanced through the alcoves into the heart of the crypt. On the floor, she found the pile of bones and rags less dusty than the rest and stooped down to paw through the remains. A sharp jolt at her fingertips told her when she had found it.

She lifted the Rune of Earthfire reverently, feeling the raw power coursing under her hands. Buried, its energies saturated the Earth, guarding and protecting; in the open air it burned free and wild, a force of destruction. Saraid glanced over at the severed head of the revenant lying apart from the body. She favoured it with a bitter smile. "No, creature, we are hardly alike."

It was almost evening when the carnage ended. The *dearg-dul* had been correct that the Death Crones knew the secret of the Guardian Runes, and now she used that knowledge as a sword of flame against the barbarians, killing many and routing the rest. She could feel the awe and terror of her sisters watching from the temple walls, but their reactions no longer mattered to her. There was only one thing left for her to do within the temple. She sought her chamber and descended the stone steps.

"Ssister ... ssister!" The crypts were filled with creaking and moaning.

The dead were agitated, as she knew they would be. This time, however, the movements in the alcoves did not dismay her. The mouldering figures had been Death Crones before her and their fears were her fears. She knew their hunger and how to use it. She wanted no curse of the dead following her.

She stood among the crypts and called out, "Release me." The words echoed off the stone walls. "A clean death for all of you if you release me."

"Releassse..."

She was not sure whether the word was an answer, but she knew she had touched the core of their undying hunger. Was this, after all, what the generations in the crypts had waited for? A Death Crone to use the ancient Rune to break the chain of necromancy.

"Yes, release," Saraid repeated. "Let the temple survive if it can without an Old Mother. And from this day forward, let the dead rest."

Fire spurted from the scrolled amulet to cleanse the alcoves of the rotting flesh that chained the spirits of her long-dead sisters. Wisps of hair and shroud ignited like tapers, illuminating bones as they crumbled to dust. From alcove to alcove she moved, cleansing. Freeing.

As she ascended the steps from the silent crypt, she smiled bitterly. In the end it was she, not the barbarians, who was the destroyer of the Old Way. And all from an undead *dearg-dul* without the wit to know what he had set in motion.

Saraid took a last look at the arched doorway to the crypts, savouring the emptiness. And strode out into the evening.

## 🕷 CLASSIC BREAK 🕷

# A GHOST STORY

MARK TWAIN

I took a large room, far up Broadway, in a huge old building whose upper stories had been wholly unoccupied for years, until I came. The place had long been given up to dust and cobwebs, to solitude and silence. I seemed groping among the tombs and invading the privacy of the dead, that first night I climbed up to my quarters. For the first time in my life a superstitious dread came over me; and as I turned a dark angle of the stairway and an invisible cobweb swung its lazy woof in my face and clung there, I shuddered as one who had encountered a phantom.

I was glad enough when I reached my room and locked out the mould and the darkness. A cheery fire was burning in the grate, and I sat down before it with a comforting sense of relief. For two hours I sat there, thinking of bygone times; recalling old scenes, and summoning half-forgotten faces out of the mists of the past; listening, in fancy, to voices that long ago grew silent for all time, and to once familiar songs that nobody sings now. And as my reverie softened down to a sadder and sadder pathos, the shrieking of the winds outside softened to a wail, the angry beating of the rain against the panes diminished to a tranquil patter, and one by one the noises in the street subsided, until the hurrying footsteps of the last belated straggler died away in the distance and left no sound behind.

The fire had burned low. A sense of loneliness crept over me. I arose and undressed, moving on tiptoe about the room, doing stealthily what I had to do, as if I were environed by sleeping enemies whose slumbers it would be fatal to break. I covered up in bed, and lay listening to the rain and wind and the faint creaking of distant shutters, till they lulled me to sleep.

I slept profoundly, but how long I do not know. All at once I found myself awake, and filled with a shuddering expectancy. All was still. All but my own heart — I could hear it beat. Presently the bedclothes began to slip away slowly toward the foot of the bed, as if some one were pulling them! I could not stir; I could not speak. Still the blankets slipped deliberately away, till my breast was uncovered. Then with a great effort I seized them and drew them over my head. I waited, listened, waited. Once more that steady pull began, and once more I lay torpid a century of dragging seconds till my breast was naked again. At last I roused my energies and snatched the covers back to their place and held them with a strong grip. I waited. By and by I felt a faint tug, and took a fresh grip. The tug strengthened to a steady strain — it grew stronger and stronger. My hold parted, and for the third time the blankets slid away. I groaned. An answering groan came from the foot of the bed! Beaded drops of sweat stood upon my forehead. I was more dead than alive. Presently I heard a heavy footstep in my room — the step of an elephant, it seemed to me — it was not like anything human. But it was

44

moving *from* me — there was relief in that. I heard it approach the door — pass out without moving bolt or lock — and wander away among the dismal corridors, straining the floors and joists till they creaked again as it passed — and then silence reigned once more.

When my excitement had calmed, I said to myself, "This is a dream — simply a hideous dream." And so I lay thinking it over until I convinced myself that it *was* a dream, and then a comforting laugh relaxed my lips and I was happy again. I got up and struck a light; and when I found that the locks and bolts were just as I had left them, another soothing laugh welled in my heart and rippled from my lips. I took my pipe and lit it, and was just sitting down before the fire, when — down went the pipe out of my nerveless fingers, the blood forsook my cheeks, and my placid breathing was cut short with a gasp! In the ashes on the hearth, side by side with my own bare footprint, was another, so vast that in comparison mine was but an infant's! Then I had *had* a visitor, and the elephant tread was explained.

I put out the light and returned to bed, palsied with fear. I lay a long time, peering into the darkness, and listening. Then I heard a grating noise overhead, like the dragging of a heavy body across the floor; then the throwing down of the body, and the shaking of my windows in response to the concussion. In distant parts of the building I heard the muffled slamming of doors. I heard, at intervals, stealthy footsteps creeping in and out among the corridors, and up and down the stairs. Sometimes these noises approached my door, hesitated, and went away again. I heard the clanking of chains faintly, in remote passages, and listened while the clanking grew nearer — while it wearily climbed the stairways, marking each move by the loose surplus of chain that fell with an accented rattle upon each succeeding step as the goblin that bore it advanced. I heard muttered sentences; half-uttered screams that seemed smothered violently; and the swish of invisible garments, the rush of invisible wings. Then I became conscious that my chamber was invaded — that I was not alone. I heard sighs and breathings about my bed, and mysterious whisperings. Three little spheres of soft phosphorescent light appeared on the ceiling directly over my head, clung and glowed there a moment, and then dropped — two of them upon my face and one upon the pillow. They spattered, liquidly, and felt warm. Intuition told me they had turned to gouts of blood as they fell — I needed no light to satisfy myself of that. Then I saw pallid faces, dimly luminous, and white uplifted hands, floating bodiless in the air — floating a moment and then disappearing. The whispering ceased, and the voices and the sounds, and a solemn stillness followed. I waited and listened. I felt that I must have light or die. I was weak with fear. I slowly raised myself toward a sitting posture, and my face came in contact with a clammy hand! All strength went from me apparently, and I fell back like a stricken invalid. Then I heard the rustle of a garment — it seemed to pass to the door and go out.

When everything was still once more, I crept out of bed, sick and feeble, and lit the gas with a hand that trembled as if it were aged with a hundred years. The light brought some little cheer to my spirits. I sat down and fell into a dreamy contemplation of that great footprint in the ashes. By and by its outlines began to waver and grow dim. I glanced up and the broad gas flame was slowly wilting away. In the same moment I heard that elephantine tread again. I noted its approach, nearer and nearer, along the musty halls, and dimmer and dimmer the light waned. The tread reached my very door and paused — the light had dwindled to a sickly blue, and all things about me lay in a spectral twilight. The door did not open, and yet I felt a faint gust of air fan my cheek, and presently was conscious of a huge, cloudy presence before me. I watched it with fascinated eyes. A pale glow stole over the Thing; gradually its cloudy folds took shape — an arm appeared, then legs, then a body, and last a great sad face looked out of the vapour. Stripped of its filmy housings, naked, muscular and comely, the majestic Cardiff Giant loomed above me!

All my misery vanished — for a child might know that no harm could come with that benignant countenance. My cheerful spirits returned at once, and in sympathy with them the gas flamed up brightly again. Never a lonely outcast was so glad to welcome company as I was to greet the friendly giant. I said:

"Why, is it nobody but you? Do you know, I have been scared to death for the last two or three hours? I am most honestly glad to see you. I wish I had a chair — here, here, don't try to sit down in that thing!"

But it was too late. He was in it before I could stop him, and down he went — I never saw a chair shivered so in my life.

"Stop, stop, You'll ruin ev—"

Too late again. There was another crash, and another chair was resolved into its original elements.

"Confound it, haven't you got any judgment at all? Do you want to ruin all the furniture in the place? Here, here, you petrified fool—"

But it was no use. Before I could arrest him he had sat down on the bed, and it was a melancholy ruin.

"Now what sort of a way is that to do? First you come

lumbering about the place bringing a legion of vagabond goblins along with you to worry me to death, and then when I overlook an indelicacy of costume which would not be tolerated anywhere by cultivated people except in a respectable theatre, and not even there if the nudity were of *your* sex, you repay me by wrecking all the furniture you can find to sit down on. And why will you? You damage yourself as much as you do me. You have broken off the end of your spinal column, and littered up the floor with chips of your hams till the place looks like a marble yard. You ought to be ashamed of yourself — you are big enough to know better."

"Well, I will not break any more furniture. But what am I to do? I have not had a chance to sit down for a century." And the tears came into his eyes.

"Poor devil," I said, "I should not have been so harsh with you. And you are an orphan, too, no doubt. But sit down on the floor here — nothing else can stand your weight — and besides, we cannot be sociable with you away up there above me; I want you down where I can perch on this high counting-house stool and gossip with you face to face."

So he sat down on the floor, and lit a pipe which I gave him, threw one of my red blankets over his shoulders, inverted my sitz-bath on his head, helmet fashion, and made himself picturesque and comfortable. Then he crossed his ankles, while I renewed the fire, and exposed the flat, honey-combed bottoms of his prodigious feet to the grateful warmth.

"What is the matter with the bottom of your feet and the back of your legs, that they are gouged up so?"

"Infernal chilblains — I caught them clear up to the back of my head, roosting out there under Newell's farm. But I love the place; I love it as one loves his old home. There is no peace for me like the peace I feel when I am there."

We talked along for half an hour, and then I noticed that he looked tired, and spoke of it. "Tired?" he said. "Well, I should think so. And now I will tell you all about it, since you have treated me so well. I am the spirit of the Petrified Man that lies across the street there in the Museum. I am the ghost of the Cardiff Giant. I can have no rest, no peace, till they have given that poor body burial again. Now what was the most natural thing for me to do, to make men satisfy this wish? Terrify them into it! Haunt the place where the body lay! So I haunted the museum night after night. I even got other spirits to help me. But it did no good, for nobody ever came to the museum at midnight. Then it occurred to me to come over the way and haunt this place a little. I felt that if I ever got a hearing I must succeed, for I had the most efficient company that perdition could furnish. Night after night we have shivered around through these mildewed halls, dragging chains, groaning, whispering, tramping up and down stairs, till, to tell you the truth, I am almost worn out. But when I saw a light in your room tonight I roused my energies again and went at it with a deal of the old freshness. But I am tired out — entirely fagged out. Give me, I beseech you, give me some hope!"

I lit off my perch in a burst of excitement, and exclaimed:

"This transcends everything — everything that ever did occur! Why you poor blundering old fossil, you have had all your trouble for nothing — you have been haunting a *plaster cast* of yourself — the real Cardiff Giant is in Albany!

"Confound it, don't you know your own remains?"

I never saw such an eloquent look of shame, of pitiable humiliation, overspread a countenance before.

The Petrified Man rose slowly to his feet, and said:

"Honestly, *is* that true?"

"As true as I am sitting here."

He took the pipe from his mouth and laid it on the mantel, then stood irresolute a moment (unconsciously, from old habit, thrusting his hands where his pantaloons pockets should have been, and meditatively dropping his chin on his breast), and finally said:

"Well — I *never* felt so absurd before. The Petrified Man has sold everybody else, and now the mean fraud has ended by selling its own ghost! My son, if there is any charity left in your heart for a poor friendless phantom like me, don't let this get out. Think how *you* would feel if you had made such an ass of yourself."

I heard his stately tramp die away, step by step down the stairs and out into the deserted street, and felt sorry that he was gone, poor fellow — and sorrier still that he had carried off my red blanket and my bath tub.

# DEPTHS

C. I. KEMP

It's been years since Randy Hellinger disappeared. Some people say that he's dead and that the body will never be found. Others say he's entered the Witness Protection Program and is living somewhere else under a different name. Some say he's gone underground.

Gone underground. That's almost funny.

"Beam us down, Mr. Scott."

A crackle of electricity; two human forms disappear then reappear at the base of a rocky outcropping.

"Tricorder readings, Mr. Spock."

"Confirming atmospheric conditions similar to earth, Captain; 30% oxygen, 12% nitrogen, 8% hydrogen, remainder unclassified inert elements. Geology comprised of bedrock, mostly iron ore or variations thereof. No fault lines. Stable."

"Life forms?"

"Readings indicate close proximity. Non-carbon based.

Distinctly non-human."

"Their intentions, Mr. Spock?"

"Insufficient data, Captain. Tricorder readings indicate they are approaching rapidly."

"Set phasers to stun."

"Tricorder readings indicate an anomaly, Captain. It would appear — HOLY CROW!"

Anomaly, indeed.

On the day Randy and I discovered it, I was a ten-year-old playing Captain Kirk. Randy, same age, was Mr. Spock.

"HOLY CROW!"

I saw it the same time Randy did. We were staring at the rock face of Morgan's Bluff, at something which wasn't there yesterday, or the day before, or any of the countless days before.

A hole. An opening in the face of a rocky wall, every inch of which was familiar to us. At least, until then.

I stood there, while Randy, the more daring, but with the same goofy, open-mouthed expression of wonder I must have had, moved closer.

The opening was maybe two or three inches higher than the top of Randy's head, as he stepped through. I wanted to warn him not to go any further, but I couldn't make my mouth form words.

Randy had no such trepidation. "Hey, Denny! Come here! You gotta see this!"

I don't know how I summoned up the courage to follow him. I walked under the arch and stood next to my best friend, saw what he was seeing, and gaped, just as he was gaping.

It wasn't just a hole. It was a cave, birthed overnight. Facing us was a passage which curved off to one side and downward. Randy took a few steps forward, and I followed him, gingerly. As we walked farther into the cave, the heat of the summer air gave way to a refreshing coolness, like an air-conditioned room. We walked on, until the light from the opening faded. The passage sloped downward, narrowing. The only way you could keep going was to crawl on your belly.

I started to back away, but Randy grabbed my arm "Man! This is so cool!"

"You're not thinking of going down there, are you?"

"Heck, yeah! Aren't you?"

"No way, man! This is crazy! Come on, Randy! This place wasn't here yesterday! This is crazy!"

"Who cares? This is so cool!"

"But you can't see a thing down there! How do you know you won't fall into a bottomless pit or something?"

Randy paused and I thought I'd gotten through to him. Then he yelled, "Come on!" He pushed me toward the cave entrance. When we were both outside, he started running.

"Where are we going?" I yelled, trying to keep up with him.

"You'll see!"

By the time we got back to Randy's house, he hadn't even broken a sweat. I was puffing hard, trying to catch my breath and ignore the stitch in my side.

"Come on!"

"No, I'll wait out here," I said and collapsed on his front steps, still puffing from the run. Randy didn't say anything, but ran into the house.

I was just as glad to let Randy think I was hanging outside because I was tired. Truth was, I was afraid to go into that house. Randy's real dad left Morgan's Crossing when Randy was two and his mum had had a string of boyfriends since then. She ended up marrying this guy,

53

Bill. Randy always said Bill was no kind of nice guy. I believed it. Many times, I'd seen Randy with a shiner under one eye or the frames of his glasses fixed with a piece of adhesive tape. Bill had always been civil to me, if you can call an occasional grunt being civil. I knew what his temper was like, though. The last thing I wanted was to be on the receiving end of it. So I waited outside.

A few seconds later, Randy came out holding an enormous flashlight. "Come on!" he yelled.

"Okay, okay, but no running this time."

"Wuss."

On the way back to the bluff, I kept hoping that the cave would just disappear. I wanted things to go back to the way they were before. To Randy, this all might seem new and exciting, but to me, it was scary and unnatural. Yet, I knew, as long as I was in Randy's presence, I'd be swept up in the excitement. Any good sense I might have would yield to his high energy and enthusiasm. The prospect frightened me, but it also thrilled me a little.

When we got back to the bluff, the cave was still there. Randy went first, turning on the flashlight and aiming it forward. We got to the spot inside the cave where we'd stopped earlier, Randy got on his belly, then snaked his body through the opening. I squatted on the ground, trying to follow his progress. The ground was damp and cold, and felt like moist clay. After Randy's feet disappeared, I could see the glow from the flashlight, growing dimmer as he moved further away from me until it went out altogether.

"Randy?"

No answer.

I counted to ten before I shouted again. Again, no answer. I yelled a third time.

This time, I heard, "Denny!"

"Randy! Are you okay?"

"Denny, you gotta come down here! This is so awesome!"

Against my better judgment, I got down on my belly and peered into the passage. "I can't see anything!"

"Here, wait!" Randy aimed the light in my direction. I could see that the passage sloped down and to the left. It was a gentle incline, but tight, one that Randy could negotiate without difficulty. I wasn't so sure about myself.

"I don't know, Randy..."

"Aw, come on!"

Taking a deep breath, I edged myself down into the opening, head first.

It was narrow, all right, and here I was, chunky, awkward, unathletic me, squeezing into a hole which skinny, gangling Randy could make it through with no trouble. I managed to keep from being wedged in there only by keeping my arms straight out in front and inching forward using my elbows, and pushing myself with my feet. Every so often, I'd find a hand-hold on the floor or the walls of the passage and use it to move myself onward. It was slow going. The passage was narrow, sometimes wet. Rocks jutted out from the ceilings and the walls. I had to contort my body in strange and unnatural ways to get past them. Movement was always possible, the twists and turns were gradual, and before long, the passage widened and opened into a larger chamber.

This was where Randy was, squatting on the ground, aiming the flashlight in my direction. When I came through the passage we both stood up and examined our surroundings.

It was a large circular chamber with a diameter of about forty feet. There were stalactites hanging from the ceiling which was about twenty feet high. The walls were covered with smooth, polished flowing shapes which looked like they'd been frozen in mid-flow. Randy nudged me and pointed at something towards the ceiling. At first, I couldn't see what it was, but then my eye caught movement. There were bats flying around up there. I looked over at Randy and he was grinning big time. I was too.

He was right — this place was awesome!

How the cave got there was something we'd never figure out. At first, I thought there might have been some kind of earthquake or maybe some shift in the ground. The shift or earthquake caused this cave, hidden all these years, to open up overnight. Even as it occurred to me, though, I realised how dumb that sounded.

Nor did we ever find out why we were the only ones it appeared to. You better believe that if a cave opened up overnight, out of nowhere, people in Morgan's Crossing would be talking about it. No one ever did, though, because no one else knew about it, and that's something else we'd never figure out. Anyway, after a while, familiarity bred contempt, and I stopped being afraid of the cave.

All we knew was we'd been presented with a secret place which was ours, ours alone, for we swore never to tell anyone else about it. Why would we? We were a pair of misfits: gawky, bespectacled Randy with his Dumbo ears, and jowly me, carrying baby fat like it was crazy-glued to me. Taunted by our age-mates and victims of numerous beatings from bullies like Ricky Pulver, Randy and I were bonded to each other, courtesy of the differences which set us apart us from the other kids.

There were two more features of this cave I have to tell you about. One, I discovered on my own one day coming home from school. I'd gotten word that Ricky Pulver was looking for me, and I knew what that meant. So instead of going home from school the usual way, I decided to go by way of Morgan's Bluff.

When I got there, the cave was gone.

It had been there the day before, and the day before that, and the day before that, and now it was gone. I felt my eyes start to tear, worse than if I'd gotten that beating from Ricky Pulver. I turned and ran in the direction of Randy's house. I had to let him know.

When I got there and told him, he looked at me like I'd grown two heads. "You're nuts! I was there this morning!"

"No, it's gone! I swear!"

"I'll betcha!"

"What?"

"Ten bucks!"

I'd gotten ten dollars from my grandmother for my birthday. I hadn't spent it yet; it was still in my dresser drawer. "Okay. Ten bucks!"

"Let's go!"

I went with Randy back to the bluff, certain that by day's end, I'd have twenty bucks in my dresser drawer.

I ended up ten dollars poorer.

The other discovery came when Randy and I were playing *Star Trek* in the circular chamber. By this time, we had stashed several flashlights, batteries, and six-packs of Coke which stayed cold in the cool air. Or rather, Randy had stashed all this stuff. I offered to go halves with him on it, but he told me not to worry, it was on him. I shrugged it off, not realising what we'd have to deal with later on.

But first, I have to tell you about the Klingon.

There was no end of games we played in the narrow passages of our cave or in that big chamber. We were heroes chasing gangsters, super-villains, aliens. We were Frank and Joe Hardy, the Lone Ranger and Tonto, Superman, Batman, Spider Man...

The day we saw the Klingon, we were Kirk and Spock again. The chamber was a Klingon outpost, the bats overhead were Klingon starships. We were surrounded by hostile Klingons, blasting them with our flashlights, doubling as phasers, awaiting rescue from the Enterprise. In our scenario, we were trapped, facing certain death, the charges in our phasers all but gone, yet there we were, ready to make our climactic, heroic stand.

We were discussing strategy when we heard something in the direction of the narrow passage leading into our chamber. We froze, listening, and heard it again. There was no mistake; it was a footstep.

We turned our flashlights in the direction of the noise, and I saw it.

A Klingon. Big, muscular, towering, with the furrows in the forehead and the bridge of the nose. Thick black brows forming a sinister V over the eyes. Black bristle-brush hair covering its head, and flowing downward along the cheeks and across the chin. Brown, reptilian skin. Holding a spearlike weapon, facing us, mouth drawn emitting an ominous, guttural snarl. Coming toward us. Mean, ugly, dangerous.

For real.

I wanted to run, but there was nowhere to run to. The chamber was a closed cul-de-sac except for the one passage which led into it, and which was now blocked.

Randy wasn't scared, though. As soon as the Klingon appeared, Randy aimed his phaser ... flashlight ... in its direction, yelled "Fire!" and made a "Zzzttt" kind of noise. No sooner had he done so than the Klingon disappeared, just like that.

I stood there for maybe a split second, shaking, starting to cry, and then I made a beeline for the tunnel. I was getting out of there. Randy came after me. "Hey, Denny, what's the matter?"

"What do you mean, 'What's the matter?'" I shouted back. "This place stinks! We could have been killed! We have no business being here! I'm going!"

Randy grabbed my arm. I pushed him away and shouted, "What's the matter with you? That thing could have killed us!" and launched into a graphic description of the Klingon, right down to the funky-looking spear it was carrying.

Randy just stared at me, as if I were the alien species. When I was done, he said, "You saw it?"

"Yeah, I saw it! You telling me you didn't?"

Randy kept staring at me, wide-eyed, unbelieving. "You're not goofing on me? You really saw it?"

"I saw it, Randy. It was there! Didn't you?"

"No. Well, yeah. I mean — I didn't see him, but — I

made him up. I made like he was there just like you said, but he wasn't really there." He paused. "You saw him? For real?"

I nodded, and Randy looked even more disbelieving and I guess I did too. Was it possible? Could something you imagined become real in this place? Well, why not? This was a cave that came and went, appearing only to us, with no logical explanation, so couldn't other fantastic things happen once you were inside it? I was pondering these questions when I realised that Randy was shaking me and saying something.

"What?"

"Try it."

"Try what?"

"Make up something. See if we can see it."

I wanted to refuse, but I couldn't. Countering my fear was my own curiosity plus the voice and demeanour of my best friend. He wasn't scared, he was delighted. Everything that was happening was one big, glorious adventure, and he wanted for me to be part of it.

"Okay," I hesitated, and thought back to my favourite *Star Trek* episode. It was the one where Kirk is on a hostile planet in a fight to the death with an alien who looks like a lizard. I closed my eyes and pictured the lizard-man, clear and distinct. Big and bulky. Dinosaur head with a scaly horn-thing on top. Mouth and teeth like a tyrannosaurus. Animal skin tunic with a weapons belt, an ugly black knife in his claw.

"Wow!"

Randy's voice shook me from my reverie. I looked where he was looking and I almost lost it.

He was there — that image from my mind's eye was facing us, hissing at us, waving that ugly black knife.

I didn't stop to think. I did what Randy did before — I aimed my flashlight at it, yelled "Fire!" and went "Zzzttt."

The lizard-man disappeared, just like that, and though I was still scared, I just started laughing. I couldn't stop.

"Don't you see, Denny?" Randy had to shout to be heard over my hysterics. "This place is ours! We're in charge here! Nothing can hurt us! We can do anything here! Anything!"

It was true. In a world of Bills and Ricky Pulvers, we'd been handed this disappearing, reappearing hole in the ground which followed its own set of rules. Our rules. We could make things happen here. Scary things. Wonderful things. Things we could never enjoy on the outside. Here...

Randy was right. From that day on, our play-acting took on a new freshness and excitement that we'd never experienced before. We were still the good guys, fighting enemy agents, ninjas, monsters, you name it. Only now, they weren't make-believe phantasms which only existed in our minds; they were real, they were solid, and they were at our mercy. They appeared, and then disappeared at our whim. Randy was right - it was awesome.

Until it started to go bad.

Over the next couple of years, we outgrew the play-acting games, but we still enjoyed hanging out in the cave. It wasn't until one day in my twelfth year, that I got a sense as to how things were starting to change between us.

Randy was waiting for me in the circular chamber drinking something that wasn't a coke. When I squeezed my way through, he handed me a similar something and said "Have one."

"What's this?"

"Beer."

"Where'd you get it?"

He shrugged. "Don't worry. Just take it."

I didn't want it, but I didn't want to look bad in Randy's eyes, so I took it. It tasted horrible, but I managed to finish it. I don't think I hid my discomfort too well from Randy, though. He seemed pretty amused.

Another time, I got down there, Randy was puffing on a cigarette, in fact, there was a whole carton of them lying on the floor. He offered me one. This time, I did refuse.

Still another time, he was smoking something that didn't quite smell like a cigarette. Again, he offered, again I refused. Randy didn't say anything, but I could tell that he was put out because I rebuffed his offer.

It all came to a head one day, when I went by Randy's house. I rang the doorbell and was answered, not by Randy, but by Bill, looking real ticked off.

"Come inside, Dennis. I want to talk to you."

He ushered me into the living room, and I was feeling all nervous and worried. I'd knew about Bill's temper and how mean he could get when he'd been drinking, which he was. It was pretty obvious.

Randy was sitting on the couch looking sullen, and I guessed that he and Bill were having words before I got there. Bill gestured for me to sit next to Randy, and I wasn't about to argue.

"Dennis, I caught Randy taking money out my wallet just now. I've also been noticing other things of mine have gone missing around the house. Do you know anything about this?"

I thought of our stash back at the cave, and more

recently, about the beer and the smokes. I'd only half wondered where they'd come from, maybe even suspected a little, but now I knew for sure. Randy had been ripping off his stepfather, and things were about to hit the fan.

"I asked you a question, Dennis," Bill said, raising his voice. "Do you know anything about this?"

I was pondering whether to speak out of fear or lie out of loyalty, when Randy shouted, "Leave him alone! He doesn't know anything! Yeah, I took the stuff!"

"Where is it?" Bill demanded.

Randy sat there, stone-faced and silent.

"Where is it?" Bill thundered, and I jumped.

"I'll show you where it is," Randy answered. "I'll take you there. Just leave Denny out of this."

Bill turned to me. "You'd better be getting on home."

I got.

I'm sure you can guess what happened next. If you think that's the end of it, though, you're wrong.

My folks gave me the word the next morning. Randy and his step-dad had gone out the day before. In the late afternoon, Randy had come running home, hysterical, saying that something had attacked his step-dad by Morgan's Bluff. They tried to get more out of him, but all he could say was that something big had jumped them, and that he had started running, but Bill...

The sheriff and a group of men headed out and found what was left of Bill. Bill's face wasn't a face anymore; it was more like bone surrounded by raw hamburger. There was a hole in his chest, or rather, a hole where his chest should have been. Only his right leg was still attached to his torso, his remaining limbs were strewn up to twenty feet away from the body. Except for his left foot. That, they never found.

You can bet that there was talk about what could do this to a man. Some said a bear, some said a big cat, a cougar maybe. One of the old timers, though, claimed that there hadn't been a bear or a big cat in or around Morgan's Crossing since he'd been living here, but no one paid him any mind. After all, it had to be some kind of big animal that could do such a world of hurt on a big strapping guy like Bill. Thank God it didn't get the boy.

Randy was no help. Every time someone asked him about it, he'd get all incoherent and talk about something big, (no, he didn't get a good look at it, he just ran) start crying, until no one had the heart to put him through any more questions. They just went out and beat the woods behind Morgan's Bluff and surrounding areas looking for something big enough and mean enough to have done this terrible thing. Of course, they found nothing.

Not even a cave by Morgan's Bluff.

I knew, though. I knew how much Randy hated Bill. He would often talk about how he'd like to take a baseball bat to Bill while he was asleep. He never did, of course, but even if he had, I don't suppose it would have made any difference, not between us.

I also knew, from our role-playing how good an actor Randy could be. It would be no stretch for him to convince the townsfolk that he'd seen something terrible and was too broken up to talk about it.

And I knew something else. Something which saddened me.

Randy had violated our pact; he'd used our private,

beautiful place for something terrible. This gift which was inexplicably bestowed upon us for the express purpose of pleasure and enjoyment had been twisted into an instrument of horror. I knew I could never enjoy another minute in that cave and I was angry that something wonderful had been wrested away from me.

There was also something else. I was becoming afraid of Randy. The boy who was once my best friend was changing. It was obvious that he was becoming more disdainful of me because I didn't like drinking beer or smoking weed. Sure, he and I had always ragged on each other. Friends do that; it's all good-natured fun, but now, Randy's gibes seemed less good-natured. When we disagreed on things, which was often, his insults seemed more like true, cruel words spoken in ill-disguised jest. We were drifting apart, not so much friends, as semi-amiable acquaintances, becoming less amiable. I could envision a day where his intolerance might be the match which burned a bridge that could never be rebuilt. What then? After seeing what happened to Bill, what then?

I vowed that I would never go back to the cave with him. That meant we could never be friends again.

Fall came, and I entered Middle School in the north end of town. I saw little of Randy; he was in a different school district. Over the next few years, we saw less of each other, but in Morgan's Crossing, paths cross whether you want them to or not. Because I saw him so infrequently, the changes were striking. He'd lost that gawkiness he'd had as a kid, replaced the skinniness with muscularity and definition. He stopped wearing the glasses and carried himself with an assurance he'd never exhibited while Bill was alive. He paraded with an arrogant cockiness, started hanging with a bad crowd, was never seen without a pack of smokes, or, in later years, the company of some trashy-looking girl.

By the time I entered high school, I'd experienced a growth spurt, dropped twenty pounds, and licked Ricky Pulver once and for all. By my senior year, I filled out a bunch of college applications before deciding on going to State, lost my virginity to Linda Greene (and vice versa), became a star player on my high school softball team with a trophy or two to show for it. I graduated State and married Linda, who helped put me through grad school. I got my Master's Degree and a good job, and then returned the favour by helping put Linda through law school. By the time we were in our early thirties, I was employed doing computer graphics, happy in my work, and Linda was working in the DA's office.

Not once in all those years did I revisit Morgan's Bluff.

Linda and I were sitting at home one night, talking about our day, when she asked me if I remembered Randy Hellinger. I said, sure, why?

That's when Linda brought me up to date. Seems Randy had fallen into some bad company: the Corey brothers. There was a name I hadn't heard in years. Bad though Bill and Ricky Pulver were, they didn't come close to the Coreys. Anything dirty that happened in Morgan's Crossing, you could lay at their door. Maybe you wanted drugs or guns that couldn't be traced. Maybe you wanted to burn down an old folks' home for the insurance money. Maybe you wanted someone beaten within an inch of their life or beyond. All you had to do was whisper a word in a Corey ear and lay down some green in a Corey palm, and the deed was done.

Randy Hellinger had gotten in deep with the Coreys. According to Linda, the DA was conducting a major investigation into organized crime in the area. And who do you suppose had been entrapped in a drug deal? None other than my onetime best friend who, in exchange for immunity from prosecution, had agreed to turn state's evidence against the Coreys.

There was just one problem: Randy was nowhere to be found.

Whether he was having second thoughts and had gone into hiding or whether the Coreys had gotten to him, no one knew.

It's funny how time can mellow your moods. Years ago, I'd come to hate and fear Randy. Now, thinking of the trouble he was in, I couldn't help remembering the good times. Even before we'd discovered the cave, each of us was the other's only refuge against waves of scorn and exclusion from our peers. In those days, though I never would have used the word, I loved him. He was the friend whose countless hours of companionship rescued me from what would have been intolerable isolation and loneliness.

Now, I hated myself for having judged him so harshly, for abandoning him as I did. Worse, I wondered if I had remained friends with him, would he have gravitated towards the bad company that led him to his current state?

It came to me in a flash. I knew where Randy Hellinger could be found.

The next day, I drove my car to the side of a road I hadn't seen since childhood, and started walking towards Morgan's Bluff. I could no more stop myself from walking towards that place now than I could years ago, even though I'd been so scared. I wasn't scared now, but I was driven by something stronger than fear. Guilt? Remorse? Nostalgia? I didn't stop to think about it, I just went.

When I got there, I saw the cave. I guess it was what I expected to see, for I'd brought the flashlight I keep in my glove compartment for emergencies. I crouched down, and walked into the entrance.

It was pretty much as I remembered it. At the very point where you could no longer see the daylight, the passage sloped downward and narrowed. I got down on my belly and called out:

"Randy? Are you down there?"

There was no answer.

I turned on the flashlight and aimed the beam down the gentle sloping aperture and eased myself down. It seemed less narrow than I remembered, but I also recalled how chunky and out-of-shape I'd been the last time I did this. It was with greater ease that I was able to elbow my way down and push myself with my feet. I used the same hand-holds to keep moving forward. I negotiated the same twists and turns, contorted myself past the same jutting rocks, surprised at how familiar it was after all these years. Soon, the passage would widen and I'd be in the large, domed circle-like chamber.

That's when I heard the noise.

It was low at first, and I wasn't sure where it was coming from. I thought it was the sound of my own body, scraping against the cave floor as I moved forward. When I stopped, it continued, and I noted that it had an ominous organic quality to it.

It was a growl, low and menacing, and with it was the sound of something soft, clicking, coming closer. The sound of claws padding on clay. I aimed the flashlight ahead of me, to see what lay beyond, listening to the sound of growls and clicking becoming louder, coming closer. All at once something knocked the light out of my hands and I was in absolute darkness. I felt a warm, foul stench breathed into my face, and saw a pair of hideous reddish eyes, inches from my own!

"Randy!" I yelled. "It's me! It's Denny! Can you hear me?"

For a second or two, the growls continued, and then stopped.

The eyes disappeared.

"Denny?"

"Yeah! Randy, is that you? Are you okay?"

For a moment, there was more silence, and I wondered if he heard me. I fumbled around in the dark for the flashlight.

I heard footsteps and let myself be guided by them. I eased myself out of the passage into that final chamber in the dark. It was as if it had only been days, rather than decades, when I'd last done this.

I felt Randy's cold hand reach for mine. We grasped hands in unison, and then embraced, and I recoiled. Even in the dark, I could tell something was horribly wrong. Randy, who had begun to bulk up when I'd last seen him, was now more skinny and wasted than when we were kids. He was wearing some kind of thick cotton shirt, but even through the thickness, I could feel the bones. It was like hugging a skeleton.

I'd found the flashlight, turned it on, and saw him for

the first time in over a decade: sick, wasted, and shambling. Decayed, and desiccated from long years of drug abuse and worse. Chalky shards of skin, broken only by red pock marks, oozing with something gross and puslike.

"I'm glad you came, Denny," he was saying. "I've screwed up really bad. I don't know how I let things get..." That's when he started sobbing.

I found myself sobbing, too. "Listen, Randy, I know about the Coreys. Come on back with me. My wife works for the DA. Let us help you. We can..."

"No, you can't. Listen, Denny, even if I go with you, I'm dead whether the Coreys get to me or not. You don't know some of the things I've done to screw up my life, and there isn't time to go into it. You've got to go, Denny. And you've got to go quick."

"Randy, I'm sorry..."

"No! It's not your fault. You've always been a damn good friend. But you have to go, Denny. You have to go *now*! Don't you hear that?"

I listened and I did hear it. A sound, not of growling or of paws padding on soft earth, but a different sound, soft and inexorable. The sound of rock scraping against rock, very, very slowly. I heard it and I knew.

"Good bye, Denny. Thanks for everything."

"Good bye, Randy."

I scrambled through the narrow passage that would lead me back to daylight, my worst fears being realised. Once again, I was a fat little boy, forcing my way through a passage that was too tight for me and getting tighter by the minute. I struggled - getting out was harder than getting in, only partially because I was going up, not down, working against gravity, not with it. There were no growls this time, but the tunnel seemed alive, holding me, constricting me. Still, I moved forwards, my shirt and jeans ripping against the jagged surface of the rock as it tightened against me. In my mind, I shrieked a desperate prayer as I struggled forward, listening as the now cacophonous scraping of rock against rock assaulted my ears.

Finally, I emerged from the sloping passage and was able to stand. Still, I had to edge my way sideways towards the entrance, as the passage was now too narrow to accommodate me any other way. The cave entrance had once been large enough to allow a tall ten-year-old boy to pass through it; now it wasn't even big enough for a large dog. I threw myself on the ground and dove through the opening into daylight, and lay there on the hard, dry earth, panting. The back of my shirt hung from me in tatters and my back was ragged and bleeding. I had dropped the flashlight in my final leap towards freedom, and my palms were serrated and covered with muck.

When my breathing returned to normal, I got to my feet and turned around. What I saw was the rock face of Morgan's Bluff, whole and unbroken.

I never told anyone the things that happened in that cave. I wouldn't be telling them now if not for something I saw the last time I drove by Morgan's Bluff.

There were bulldozers and earth movers and a sign saying that this was going to be the site of the Morgan's Crossing Mall. That means they're also going to be blasting Morgan's Bluff, and when they do, who knows what they're

going to find?
    I don't. And to tell you the truth, I don't want to know.

# FAILED SACRIFICE

## SABRINA WEST

When the coastline disappeared behind the choppy ocean, Cecily began to panic. She'd been crazy to come out with Annie in this weather, but she hadn't been able to ignore the desperation in her best friend's voice. Now, a darker emotion gleamed in Annie's eyes as she pulled on the ropes, her breath coming in raspy pants, lips curled back over gritted teeth.

Another wave slapped against the side of the boat, drenching Cecily. But before she could ask Annie to turn back, her friend cleated the mainsail, secured the rudder, and leaned over to speak to her.

"Thank you for coming. I'm sorry to bring you all the way out here in this weather, but I needed someone to talk to." Annie took a deep breath. "My father is dying of cancer."

"Oh no! I'm so sorry." Trying to hold herself steady through the rocking of the boat, Cecily hugged her friend.

Annie pushed her away. "There's more. He's in debt. The bank is going to foreclose on our house, and I'm not going to be able to go to college."

"Oh, Annie. Is there anything I can do to help?"

Annie put both her hands on Cecily's face and leaned in. "I was hoping you would say that."

Cecily shifted back on the bench. There was something unfamiliar in Annie's voice, a flatness that unnerved her.

Annie's eyes were bright, almost feverish. "You'd do anything for me, right Cecily?"

"Uh, yeah, of course. Hey, it's getting really choppy out here. Let's go back and talk to my parents. They'll be glad to help, I'm sure."

"It's too late for that." Annie reached into the pocket of her coat and pulled out a long silver whistle.

"Annie..."

Annie smiled, and put a finger to her lips. She raised the whistle and blew one high note.

Stillness spread out from her in a circle, calming the wind and the turbulent ocean. In a heartbeat, everything in sight turned to fog and glass-smooth water. As Annie lowered the whistle, all Cecily could hear was her own harsh breathing.

Mouth agape, she stared out at the still world. The seascape was tinged with lavender, though she couldn't tell if the colour came from the clouds or the sea reflecting it. Ocean mirrored sky out to the horizon until it was impossible to determine where one ended and the other began. A smell of acid lingered in the air, so strong that it seemed to coat her tongue.

"What is this?" asked Cecily.

"This," said Annie, "is the only way to fix things." From under the seat cover, she pulled out a long, thin filleting knife.

Cecily's heart thudded hard. "Hey, now."

Annie looked at her through wide, unblinking eyes. "Just watch." She wrapped her hand around the blade. As

74

blood trailed around her wrist, she dropped the knife and held her arm over the bow. The steady trickle of blood into the sea echoed around them.

"Look," said Annie.

Warily, Cecily leaned forward. Instead of diffusing into the grey water, Annie's blood formed a disc. A few more drops fell, and the circle began to spin, the centre sinking to form a vortex that did not disturb the water around it.

"My family is one of the ones that settled here in the 1600s, did you know that?" Annie's voice deepened to a rough lilt. "Though they barely survived the early winters, they managed to prosper. But many in the town were jealous of their success, which my ancestors were unwilling to share. In revenge, some of the families in the town formed an alliance with the sun gods.

"My ancestors, with no way to withstand the heat withering their fields, turned to the sun gods' rival: a creature from the deep ocean. The battle went on for years, but in the end, our side was victorious."

"I remember this from when we were kids," Cecily said slowly. "I was the sun god, and you were the sea monster. It was your favourite game."

"I thought it was just a story, but my grandfather told me the truth. You see, after the last of the sun gods' servants were driven out, the pact was forgotten. The ties were all but dissolved." Annie leaned forward. "Do you know what is needed, to restore what has been lost, to allow us to prosper once more?"

Dizzy with fear, from the strange landscape and the emptiness in Annie's voice, Cecily looked down at the ocean and the growing whirlpool. "Blood?"

Annie leaned in close. "Sacrifice," she whispered.

She reached out and pushed Cecily, hard. The motion

was so swift that Cecily didn't have a chance of catching a handhold. She fell straight back into icy water.

The ocean swallowed her scream. Water flowed into her mouth, into her lungs. Cecily tried to fight her way back up to the surface, but a force sucked her down through darker and colder layers of blue. Each attempt to breathe brought a sharp pain, but she refused to stop struggling.

And as the last bits of light and colour bled to black, she could no longer perceive the beating of her heart. She fell for what seemed like forever, through darkness so dense and cold that it became the only thing left in her life. The question of whether or not she lived scraped at the edges of her dazed mind. The icy cold numbed her emotions until she relaxed into the force that pressed her into stillness. After a while, she perceived a hum, a chilly energy that pulsed like her missing heartbeat.

Finally, the pull stopped. With her last bit of strength, she tried to kick upward, but the movement of her arms and legs had no effect. Water crushed her from all sides. Her movements were languid, her hand slow to brush away the hair that swirled around her face. All was black.

There, a flicker of light. Listless, she tilted her head, trying to see it more closely. The light moved out of sight. After a few moments, it appeared again. Then there was another, and another. They hovered at the edges of her vision, moving in dim, greenish trails. She peered at them, trying to make out the shapes behind the movement.

"They're always curious about new arrivals." The voice was hollow, resonant, like an off-key whale song. Fingers that tapered into fronds appeared and disappeared with the brief proximity of a green light.

Cecily tried to speak, to demand the voice tell her where she was, and how to return to the surface. But she couldn't unclench her jaws. Energy hissed across her skin, returning a semblance of life to her frozen nerves.

"This sacrifice, under the contract made hundreds of years ago, would link you to me forever. But there was a problem." Its head tilted, the movement visible if not the features.

The lights around her highlighted a sliver of white drifting down. Then came larger pieces: wood, a bit of cloth, a compass. Things that shouldn't sink. The lights drew closer together, illuminating a body that flopped like a rag doll. Annie's eyes were stark and staring as she was dragged down out of sight. Again, Cecily struggled to scream. But the magic leeched away her grief before she could process it.

"Shame to dispose of one of the blood, but her actions were unacceptable." Greenish grey skin flickered with an oily sheen, swollen in lumps and ridges of flesh. "Her ancestors were smart enough to state in our contract that none of their line can become a sacrifice, but I will not tolerate the existence of blood tainted by madness. And she was well on her way to that. So this is my qualm. I have been so long without tribute, but you are an improper, empty sacrifice."

As the lights gathered around the speaker, Cecily tried to shut her eyes, to turn her head away, but she was frozen.

A flat face with a slit for a mouth emerged from the darkness. Opaque eyes a shade darker than its skin regarded her. "You belong to me. But as you are, I cannot keep you."

*If you cannot keep me, set me free,* she shouted at it with all the mental strength she possessed. *Let me go, please. I do not want this.*

The creature's lips slid open in a mockery of a smile,

revealing rows upon rows of needlelike teeth tinged a pale orange in the dim glow. It drifted forward, raising its arm with a lazy flick of fronds. Pain sliced across her cheek as they brushed her face. With that shock, her jaws at last cracked open. Bubbles frothed from her mouth, black and oily instead of filled with air. She tried to close her mouth, but they kept coming, surrounding her in a spiral and obscuring her view of the deep. She hurtled backward, faster and faster until she at last broke the surface of the ocean.

With sand under her palms and wind tangling her sodden hair, she tried to draw in breath. Black, oily water bubbled from her lips and nose. She leaned over on her hands and knees and vomited the dark liquid. When the spasms left her, she collapsed on the beach, gasping in air. She pressed her uninjured cheek to the cool ground, and her hand slid up to the renewed beat of her heart. The other side of her face ached with a pulsing heat. When she pressed her fingers there, it was swollen and bloody, and caked with sand.

The grit of the sand scraping her skin, she pushed herself to her knees. The dark liquid coated her, making her skin slick and oily. She rubbed at her wet clothes, but it wouldn't come off. She wanted to be sick again, but there was nothing left in her.

She was amazed to be alive. Had the thing let her go? She stared out at the ocean, at the pounding surf, at the pieces of Annie's boat washing up onto the beach. The grief hit her then, doubling her over. Cecily couldn't reconcile years of memories of her best friend with the stranger who had pushed her in the ocean. It would be better to believe it had been a hallucination, but there was the oil on her skin and the fragments of the boat lining the shore.

*As you are, I cannot keep you.* She wished she knew what the creature had meant. Would she be free as long as she stayed out of the water? But the creature's words had hinted at something deeper.

*As you are...* There, just beneath the wave, was a flicker of greenish light.

Cecily turned and ran for home.

When Cecily opened the front door to her Phoenix apartment, the sound of dripping water sent panic surging through her. It had been so many years since she had encountered any sign of the creature's presence. Barely able to draw breath, she let her groceries fall to the hallway carpet. She made herself walk steadily into the kitchen. Any moment now, she would see a spreading pool of water and smell the choking salt air of the ocean. But when she peered around the corner, there was no flood, just a leaky tap plopping into the metal sink.

Cecily slid to the cracked tile, face in her shaking hands. It was okay, the creature hadn't come for her. She wouldn't have to move again. All the other occurrences were long in the past; the dead fish in her then-boyfriend's saltwater tank, the seawater bubbling up from her bathtub, the green lights drifting down the river on a cloudy night. And it had been almost as long since the last dream of cold darkness and the pressure of magic, since the creature's hollow voice had coated her thoughts. Her fingers traced the scar on her cheek, the delicate ink-black slash that refused to be concealed by makeup or fade with laser treatment.

She knew it was ridiculous to keep running. Either there

was no way the creature could catch her away from the ocean, or every body of water was hazardous. Even the rain falling from the sky could be a threat. Once she'd dreamed that the rain had dissolved her, had stripped away bits of skin, muscle and bone in an agony that had lasted all the way down river and back to the sea.

Her appetite gone, she left her groceries in the hall and went to finger the woven beads hanging in the window. She supposed it was too much to hope that she'd finally managed to drive the creature away, that purchased charms and dime-store spells had created even the most fragile barrier. But she couldn't really believe it. Though she'd searched through all the occult shops the southwest had to offer, flipped through dusty books and sketched runes in the desert sand, she'd never found even a hint of the slow thrum of magic she'd felt in the deep.

She had even sought out the sun gods that Annie had spoken of, the supposed rivals of her tormentor. She had hoped they would be eager to assist her and strike a blow to the creature from the deep, but they had disdained to send her any sort of response. That even her last resort could fail had sent her into a depression that she hadn't yet overcome, had left her hollow.

*As you are...* Fear shivered through her. She wrapped her arms against the familiar chill, breathing deep in the exercises that never truly calmed her.

Night after night, she had contemplated the meaning of its words, of what it had meant by "empty". Her frequent moves meant she was always alone, with not enough time to let friends or lovers catch hold of her. She hadn't set out to be that way. She'd just gotten tired of keeping secrets, of nurturing a fear that no one could understand.

When the mobile phone in her pocket buzzed, she

almost shrieked. With her hand to her racing heart, she frowned at the unfamiliar number on the screen, but answered anyway.

Her face grew slack as she listened to the lawyer. As he spoke of a car accident, a drunk driver and instantaneous death, she went to look out the window at the endless rows of apartments around her.

She had grown distant from her parents since she'd left. They had never understood her refusal to return to the home she had loved. Now she would have to return, the lawyer told her, to sign papers, arrange the funeral.

As the lawyer rambled on, Cecily watched puffy white clouds drift across the sky and wished she remembered how to cry. Surely her parents deserved at least that. But the lawyer's words fell into the hollow centre where emotion should be, and a terribly rational thought occurred to her. Here was an excuse to change. She would go back and fix everything with her parents' estate, prove to herself that fear should no longer rule her life. She was so weary of what she had become in the past years, this skittish creature that started at the slightest movement of light on water.

Besides, her parents' house was miles from the ocean. "Yes," she said. "I'll be there."

At the first sight of the sea, the near-empty bottle of rum fell from Cecily's fingers. It clunked twice on the street, and then rolled off the pavement to rest among brittle grass and dirty sand. Cecily put her hand to her forehead, trying to remember how she'd gotten here. She had been boxing up her parent's belongings, photos and drawers full of her childhood drawings. She'd gotten angry at herself and her weakness and her wasted life, and she'd gone to the liquor cabinet. After the fourth gin and tonic, a walk had seemed like an excellent idea. She'd not meant to come this way.

Reactions dulled of sense and emotion, her lip curled as she took in the trash lining the curbs, the boarded up shops and faded paint. This little coastal town hadn't fared well since she'd left it. She walked down the street, stumbling over cracks in the pavement. Down the hill, she caught a glimpse of gray-green water and the fog bank hovering over the horizon. She looked around at the empty town, and could not be sorry if it had managed to stand as a sacrifice in her place.

When she turned to leave, a man stood in the middle of the street, blocking her way up the hill. Arms hanging limply at his side, he watched her through wide, unblinking eyes.

*Just like Annie had...* Cecily rubbed her hands up and down her arms to erase the shivers. "May I help you?" she asked. She didn't recognize him from her childhood. He was as shabby as the town, with ragged, stained clothing and greasy hair. She rubbed her arms harder, not understanding how anyone could let himself get to that state. She hated nothing more than the feel of grease between her fingertips.

The man didn't answer. He began to walk toward her with quick, deliberate steps. Cecily moved back, digging in her purse for her can of mace. A gust of wind lifted the hair from her scarred cheek. The man's gaze fixed there, and he smiled.

Then she met his eyes, and there at last found the magic she'd sought for years. It sizzled across his skin, blazing out in waves like heat.

Cecily turned and ran. Her fingers brushed her pepper spray, but before she got a good grip, he tackled her. Light flashed across her vision as her forehead struck the pavement. He knelt over her, the unnatural heat of him seared her skin.

"Listen to me." He leaned closer, his greasy hair brushing hers. "Years ago, I offended a creature of the sun. Now I burn always, from the inside out." His hand pressed down on her shoulder, scorching hot. She bit her lip so that she would not scream. "It's promised to free me if I kill the one that belongs to the creature from the deep. Do you understand?"

Cecily's fingers wrapped around the can of mace. With a furious yell, she twisted around and sprayed it in his face. He reared back, cursing, and she scrambled free.

Before she got far, a wall of flames sprang up, blocking her escape. For a moment, she stared slack-jawed at the fire. Even as she fought the fear raging through her, she couldn't help feel a little cheated; she had received no gifts or defence as a sop for her torment.

Then he was on her again, his palms burning into her arms. She stomped on his foot, and when that didn't make him let go, she slammed her foot into his knee. There was a satisfying crack, but the sole of her sandal melted with the contact. At this rate, she would die just from the proximity of him. Leaving him lying on the street cursing, she kicked off her sandals and half limped, half ran away.

Her skin burnt and aching, she hid shaking in the shelter of a dying oak. The crackling of flames was all around her; it seemed he would set the whole town on fire to drive her from hiding. When the smoke became thick enough to choke, she ventured onto another street. The breeze had shifted in the afternoon heat. It now blew toward the ocean, sweeping the smoke through the streets of the town.

But when she looked down the hill, the access to the beach had not been cut off. There, the stranger's fire surged against an invisible barrier. Cecily stared at it for a moment, old fear overwhelmed by new. She knew it wouldn't be safe to go near the ocean, but she jogged down the hill anyway, legs and lungs burning with the exertion. Perhaps the creature would protect its own from its old enemies, even a lowly, failed sacrifice.

The sand on the beach scraped at her blistered foot. The fog bank hovering at the edge of the ocean was closer now, slipping over the water to touch land. She tried not to look at the fire reflecting on the waves. Surely it was hysteria that caused her to see bits of light too green to be caused by flame.

Down the harbour was the dock where many of the townspeople kept their boats. Going out on the open water was a risk; the creature could destroy her boat like it had Annie's. But it was a chance she would have to take.

Once she climbed onto the low dock, all she could hear was the slapping of water against the dock and the uneven creak of the boards beneath her feet. The fog was so dense that she smelled the new fire before she saw it. She walked to the end of the dock in a daze, passing dozens of smoking wrecks. So the exit from town had been a trap after all.

Cecily's legs gave out, her breaths escaping as choked wheezes. She glanced down at the green-grey ocean. There was no chance of swimming to freedom. The water was ice cold this time of year; she would last only minutes even if the creature didn't claim her. She tore at the rotten planks of the deck, bloodying her fingers in a desperate attempt to find a weapon, to have some chance at survival. But she knew it would be pointless to fight with something as flammable as wood.

Clouds swirled around her as the fog grew denser. She was closed in her own world, her and the pier and the ocean as her own private corner of hell. And one invader: the stranger with the touch of fire, just coming into view. The fog around him evaporated with a hiss in proximity to his heat.

Green flashes of light danced just below the surface of the water, gathering around the edge of the dock.

Cecily fought to hold onto her rage, her will to survive. But they were eroding in the quiet hiss of the fog, the slap of water against the pier, the creak of the wood heralding the stranger's approach. No matter if she jumped into the ocean or if she let him kill her, the ending would be the same.

It seemed she was finally to learn what the creature would do with her, and to discover the sensation of being nothing more than a light in a dark place. Her mind slipped back into the pattern of questions that had haunted her every night for years: how much it would hurt, if it would strip her body away, if she would retain enough consciousness to regret the life she'd only skulked through.

It was killing her to not know.

She began to laugh. This was the little niggle at the back of her mind that had kept her obsessed, never truly let her be happy. Relief coursed through her. Finally, all these questions would be answered, and she would no longer be tortured by uncertainty.

The creature had wanted her to be obsessed with thoughts of it, to devote her entire self to the certainty of sacrifice. In trying all those years to escape, she had dedicated her life to it. In this moment, she was no longer an improper sacrifice.

The lights ringed the dock now. Cecily sensed the creature approaching, its outline ringed by green lights and the hazy reflection of fire on water.

The man took his last steps to Cecily, flame flickering in his eyes. She hated him for the triumph in his gaze, but not as much as she hated herself for her desperate relief.

The creature's ice-cold fronds tangled in her hair. Its needle-sharp teeth pricked the back of her neck. The familiar chill flowed through her, and she couldn't help but relax into the languid terror she had felt in the deep.

*Yes*, it said to her. *Now, you are ready.*

# HANGMAN

## LISAMARIE LAMB

They were waiting for her in the attic. In the dark, dark attic. And they knew she was coming, of course. They always knew. They could feel her. It was time to play.

The day shouldn't have been as rain darkened as it was. Not at the beginning of September which surely was a month of gently shifting seasons, of autumn blowing in, quietly, so softly that you would barely notice until you felt the need for an extra layer, longer sleeves, a jacket. But this September was a miserable one for so many reasons, the weather only one of them.

"Don't you like your new house, your new bedroom?" asked Mrs Cooper as she plaited her daughter's hair, nipping at the knots that had formed overnight, one eye half on the toast under the grill. "Don't you like the garden?"

And the truth was, Jenny, nine years old and golden, *did* like her new house with the strange stray cat, her new bedroom with the wooden floor and the magic wardrobe, the garden which was miles and miles long and had a shaky old shed at the bottom of it. But instead of saying that, instead of telling the truth, she said nothing. She had said nothing for days now, as the time lurched on and the summer died away so definitely. She sniffed a little, her nose wrinkling painfully of its own accord, the tears desperate to fall, desperate to escape their fleshy confines. Her throat was tight and crumpled and her fingers felt numb with grief.

"Oh, bugger!" shouted Mrs Cooper as the smoke alarm sounded its shrill and sudden siren, the toast blackening and burning under the too red filament. She ran to the grill, switched it off, flapped a tea towel manically under the smoke alarm until it finally shut up and she swore under her breath. Jenny heard it, of course she did, but she still said nothing. And she had no breakfast.

They were running late as it was.

The first day of school. The first day of term. The first day back after the summer holidays. Only Jenny wasn't going back, would never go back, could only go forwards into a new world of no friends, no knowledge and nothing.

A new school.

Moving house in July, moving so far away from home, meant a new school. And Jenny was afraid. Of something. She couldn't quite grab at it, the fearful thing lurked just on the other side of her, just out of reach, just out of sight. But it was there. Jenny didn't feel ready for it, she hadn't prepared for this dread. She had known she would be nervous. She was expecting that. This, however, was more than nerves. This was bone shaking, sick making terror, and it came from the dreams.

In the dreams she never knew what it was either. It was

dark, though. The place and the thing, both were dark. Both were hungry.

She had tried to tell her parents, but they were so excited about the house — a grown up sort of excited which meant talking endlessly about making changes, painting this and extending that — and so proud to have made it to this part of town, to the good postcode and the good road names and the good school, that they didn't listen. Or they didn't hear. It didn't matter.

And so Jenny said nothing. At all. To anyone.

It was a drive to school now, no longer the puddle jumping, sunlight catching walk that Jenny and her mother had enjoyed for the past five years, no more popping into the corner shop on a Friday for an ice cream treat. Now Mrs Cooper, in a car older than she would have liked, especially compared to the others in the school car park, the Mercedes and the Audis and the big and bullying four by fours, had to drive, and Jenny had to sit and try not to feel sick. "You'll get used to it," she was told for the hundredth time, maybe the millionth. "Honestly. I promise." A lie if ever she had heard one.

They arrived without ceremony, pulling up with all the others, the starch stiff blue tunic tight against Jenny's contracting chest, the tie — a new phenomenon — strangling her, the royal blue blazer drowning her it was so big. She'd grow into it. Apparently. She wasn't convinced of that. "Bye then," said Mrs Cooper, wondering whether to get out of the car, wondering whether to walk her baby daughter through the gates and into the building. The look of shock on Jenny's face told her what she was supposed to do. But she asked anyway; "Want me to come with you? Get you settled?"

Jenny started to nod, changed her mind, nodded again.

"Yes please," she said, so quietly it was almost not said at all. Mrs Cooper heard it though, and her breaking heart mended just a little.

"Right, yes, okay, good." She smiled. Jenny smiled back, against her will. What she wanted to do was run to her mother and grab hold of her, to tell her to take her home, to take her back to her friends and her teachers and the building she knew inside out and upside down. But she didn't because she couldn't. So instead she nodded again and took her mother's outstretched hand. A truce. For now. It would last dependent on what the day would bring. It would not last.

The two, mother and daughter, both unsure, both not really having thought this through, walked steadily and together through the gate, up the sweeping driveway and towards the front door of the white, square, squat and beautiful building that used to be a house. A big house. A mansion house. And which was now where the administration offices, the headmistresses' room, and the library were housed. The rest of the school branched off in varying directions into extensions that were of varying ages. It was weird. It was so very strange. And it was dark.

That was Jenny's first impression of the place, of her new school. Darkness. Gone were the bright walls and light windows of her old school, no more pupils' paintings on the walls, no more posters or adverts or pegs. This place had walls of old students staring out in long lines, perched one above the other, it had shields and trophies and awards. It had old oaken doors and wood panelling. And it smelled. Not unpleasant. Not that. It was just an odour underlying everything. A little musty, slightly dusty, very old.

But she knew it would be like this. She knew it from her

dreams, the ones she kept having over and over again until she hardly dared to sleep. Long, dark corridors, little slats of windows high up but the light couldn't find them and couldn't get in. And she was running down them, either chasing or being chased. It didn't matter. Either way it was a bad situation and the only way out of it was to wake up. She couldn't do that in real life. She couldn't do that today if she found herself running down an endless gloomy corridor, the outside not wanting to penetrate the shadows.

These were dreams she hadn't told her mother about, even though she had asked as though she was expecting her daughter to tell her something of the nightmares. As though she knew. And Jenny wondered, as the pair of them made their unsure upright way from the front door to the registration office, whether she might not be the only one dreaming.

A knock on the heavy wooden door made it too late to ask, and Jenny wasn't sure the words would form in a way that would make any sense anyway.

"Come in."

And they went in.

"Mrs Cooper?" asked a small, round woman with heavy black eye makeup and a frozen smile. She was sitting behind a desk with an actual real proper old typewriter on it. Jenny wanted to touch it, to hear the chattering clatter of the keys, but instead she chose to hide behind her mother, letting herself be ignored, knowing it wouldn't last long.

Mrs Cooper nodded. "Yes. This is Jenny, we're—"

"Lost? They all are, my love, they all are." The woman stood, smoothed down her sage green skirt, and the smile stayed constant. "Now, let's see." She breezed past mother and daughter and a waft of an intense perfume, something familiar and so strong. It stung Jenny's nose and she sneezed, surprising everyone, making them look at her. Hidden no longer, Jenny sniffed, sighed and smiled.

The woman fluttered her leaden eyelashes in what may have passed for a wink. It was something strange and unusual, whatever it was. It felt like a warning. From what? The corridor? The dark? Something else?

Now was not the time.

The woman had picked up a folder and was leafing through it, licking her thumb and flicking the pages, snapping them over and over until she found what she was looking for. "You're in class Y5, third floor. Mrs Sanderson." She glanced at the clock. "Just in time for registration." The smile wavered. The woman wanted to say something, and Jenny wanted her to say something. But she said nothing except, "Do you want me to show you?"

Jenny nodded. "Yes please," she managed to croak out, swallowing perfume fumes. "Thank you." They would have their chat, the talk that was waiting to happen, that was immensely important, on the way.

"I'll come too," said Mrs Cooper, taking hold of Jenny's hand, patting it, clutching it. "I'd like to settle her in." As though she were five instead of nine. As though she were a baby. And yet a tiny part of Jenny was glad of it despite everything.

Even though the chat would have to wait.

There were lots of stairs and lots of doors and lots and lots of dark passageway. The woman — still no name, and no one felt it was the right time to ask — navigated them all smoothly and quickly, the Coopers trotting to keep up until they all stopped, quite suddenly, outside a door that looked the same as all the other doors but which was apparently special. Jenny felt her mother's grip tighten, and she knew she was safe. For now. But for how long?

Not long. As she opened the classroom door, she knew it was wrong. She knew it was the reason for the funny feelings, for the unease. And they knew it too. They saw. Even though she whipped her hand away from her mother's before they could have done, they saw.

They knew.

And that was that.

Jenny was marked.

She looked at the woman and saw a sadness behind the fixed grin. She had taken a wrong turn, right at the start, and it would steer her on a bad course now.

And then her mother kissed her making it all ten times better and a million times worse and Jenny's heart broke from love and fear.

"Ah, Miss Westerly, is this our new girl?" asked a terribly thin and terribly tall woman standing by a blackboard, holding a red book in her hands. "Is this Jenny Cooper? I saw her name on the register, I wondered where she was."

Jenny felt herself being ushered into the room and there she was, standing next to her new form teacher, being introduced to the class. Her peers, her colleagues. Her friends. Or perhaps not judging by the amused disdain on the faces in that room.

"Bye, darling." The last words Jenny heard her mother say before Miss Westerly closed the door and took her away.

And now it was them and her. And that smell. It was deeper up here, thicker, or maybe Miss Westerly throbbing perfume had simply masked it.

"Sit down, dear, over there." Jenny awoke from her wondering and wandered to the empty chair the teacher had nodded to. She slid in behind the desk, an old-fashioned wooden desk on wobbly legs that opened on a hinge and had a blue stained inkwell in the corner, next to the groove cut especially for pens and pencils. She liked it. It felt like it could hold secrets inside, like it could keep them safe for her. Jenny felt she might need it soon. That dream, leaving lingering unfathomable riddles in her mind.

The morning passed smoothly. Reasonably smoothly. Assembly was uncomfortable, she was singled out and introduced but no one listened. No one cared. Why should they? They already had their friends, they already had their cliques. They didn't need her. But it was painful too. Little pokes and kicks and nudges, little looks and sneers and flicks. And no one told her why. The innocent faces and averted eyes were a uniform for them.

They told her at first break. Jenny was standing by the lockers she had only just found, wondering where to get a key, when she heard the one, single word.

"You."

It wasn't a kindly voice, but it was addressing her, so she answered. "Yes?"

"You're a baby." The girl speaking was tall, broad, belonged in Jenny's class but she couldn't quite remember the name. It probably didn't matter.

"No I'm not!" The words were automatic, deny everything if it could lead to ... problems. "I'm not!"

There was a group now, but the leader started laughing first. The rest, like good soldiers, followed suit. Then a chant started up, shrieking through the locker room, "Baby, baby, baby!"

A hand caught her shoulder, shoved her around and down and she crashed face first into the thin metal door of locker number 111. She remembered thinking she would get into trouble because there was a dent in it now, and she remembered her cheek and her temple glowing red with pain, and then she was running. Out of the locker room, across the landing and plunging into the dismally dark corridor ahead. Pounding feet, heavy in brightly polished black buckled shoes, barely a grip, the occasional slip, followed her. *Not this, not this, it can't be this!* she screamed inside. But it was. She was living her dream now, the corridor, the fear, the drip, drip, drip of panic leaching out of her and into the wood covered walls.

When she realised that the footsteps had stopped, and that she was entirely alone, Jenny was lost. High up in the building, she thought she might be able to retrace her steps, but when she tried she found forks and turnings and doors that she couldn't remember being there the first time. She heard the bell calling her to class, and she wondered what the next lesson was going to be. She hoped it was geography. If she was going to miss some learning it might as well be that.

Another corner and there was a staircase in front of her. A spiral staircase, different, metallic and gleaming white against the oak. It looked cool and velvety. It looked enticing. So she climbed it.

This wasn't part of the dream.

This wasn't scary.

And at the top, although the darkness had tried to climb with her, it didn't quite make it. There was a small landing, a door and, the lord be praised, a window, large, letting the sunlight in now that the rain clouds had passed. Jenny stood on tiptoes to see out and blinked her way through the brightness. She felt warmth on her face and could see blue sky above her. She was in the right place. For what, she didn't know. But for now, it was enough to feel safe.

She turned and placed a small hand on the door. It squeaked a little, the catch not quite doing its job, and opened a crack. Emboldened, Jenny pushed harder, and the door opened further, allowing her entry into the attic. The dark, dark attic. The light had been a reprieve, that was all. A joke perhaps to persuade her to enter. And now she had.

This was where the smell came from.

It seeped out of the slatted walls and bled across the floorboards towards her. She sniffed, drew it in, let it enter her, let it become a part of her. It didn't seem too bad now she was in the midst of it, and she thought that it, and the darkness, might be a price worth paying to escape the bullies. The memory of them made her glance behind at the still open door. She wanted to close it, an irrational certainty poking her spine, making her believe that that group of bullies might appear any minute, trapping her. She knew lessons had begun. She knew she was alone. It just didn't feel like it.

A few steps into the attic, forcing herself away from the entrance, but not shutting the door, not shutting out the light completely, and Jenny realised that the eyes she felt staring, the ears that were certainly listening, *were* there. They were *definitely* there. But they weren't going to harm her. Because in the corner of the attic, in a thin shaft of light, was a group of toys. Old toys, stuffed toys, broken and bleeding stuffing onto the floor. Eyes missing, arms missing, heads missing in some cases, but still watching her. Still interested in her.

The toys were arranged around a blackboard. A small

one, a child's one, a half finished game of hangman played out on the greenish cracked surface, the letters and stickman drawn in pink chalk. _ E _ E C C A _ A _ S H. And the condemned man had one leg missing. Memory burst into Jenny's reeling mind, and the bully's name came to her, quickly, swiftly, and she was amazed she had forgotten it. REBECCA WALSH.

Jenny knew she had to leave. She knew she had to get to her lessons, and she knew that she was already in deepest, darkest trouble. Her mother was most likely on her way to the school, red-faced and puffing and muttering under the breath. But since she knew the answer…

Jenny's steps jolted as she made her way closer. The toys unnerved her, the floppy rag doll with a fixed sideways grin and black button eyes, the teddy bear whose ear was eaten away by some terrible thing, the blue pig with the teeth, the assortment of unclaimed woollen limbs and the stuffing. Everywhere. Everything was bleeding and dying.

But she had to answer the question. If she did nothing else right today, she knew she could do that. She made it, and nothing touched her, nothing grabbed her, nothing crawled brokenly from the heap of plush corpses to tear her apart.

Her chest was hurting, the fear was mounting and it took her three attempts to pick up the chalk. When she had it, she gripped it so hard that she could feel it grinding into her bones and it hurt and it could even have made her bleed but she didn't care. With no breath at all, lungs on fire and ribs about to shatter with the effort of keeping it all in, the effort of keeping alive and not dying from the fear, she scribbled the last of the letters. She pressed hard, the pain in her fingers sharp and deep now, the chalk melting onto the board, filling in the gaps. And then, although the word — the name — was complete, REBECCA WALSH written in a shaky, chalky, childish hand, Jenny lunged forward, flicked her wrist, and the hanging man was complete. Everything accounted for.

He was choking.

Jenny could hear it.

A rattling, screaming, scratching sound.

And was the drawing, just a drawing done in chalk and not real, not at all real, was it moving? Swinging from its scaffold, desperately clawing at the dusty rope around its neck? Fingernails snapping, it was too late, and the eyes that weren't there bulged, reddened, the tongue that Jenny couldn't see became thick and black and dead.

She stumbled backwards, tripped over something or nothing and she fell, bumping down on to her bottom with a thump and a groan. She held her breath. Waiting.

And there was a giggle.

But it didn't come from Jenny.

It came from the rag doll with the crooked smile.

The little girl scrambled to her feet, kicking up dust and moths and fear as her shiny shoes shot up and out. And then she was gone, the rag doll laughing at her retreat.

She slip slid down the spiral staircase and fell against something soft and perfumed as she came out of the final bend. Miss Westerly. Waiting for her. Worried.

The woman held the girl, held her so tightly that Jenny's ribs, about to explode moments before, were now ready to implode with the force of Miss Westerly's chest pressing down onto her, pumping the breath from her. "I didn't want you to go up there. I hoped you wouldn't. It's too late now, I'm so sorry." There were tears, but whose they were was difficult to tell and maybe it was both of them. It was probably both of them.

Jenny pushed herself away from Miss Westerly, but her arms were still gripped tight. She wanted to ask questions, started to ask questions, but the older woman put a finger to her lips. She shook her head. "It's too late. It's late. I've got to get you back to class."

And that was it.

Twisting, turning, just as confusing as it had been the first time, the passageways and corridors eventually led the pair to the right room. Miss Westerly knocked, opened the door. "Here's your missing girl." And Jenny went in, sat down, smiled sweetly and shook inside, wanting to cry but knowing better than to give the bullies more ammunition. Rebecca Walsh was watching her.

And because Rebecca Walsh was watching, waiting for her to do something, anything, to slip up somehow, to provide the next laugh, Jenny didn't mention anything to her parents. No way. Imagine her mother at the school, demanding to meet and scold and scream at the bully, her fingers itching to slap the pretty cheek, to protect her daughter. It was too much. It was not worth it.

So she stayed silent.

Days and days of torment, and she stayed silent. And Miss Westerly sometimes looked at her in that way she had, her heavy eyelids flickering with a sort of grief, a kind of sorrow. But no one asked her what was wrong, and no one asked if they could help.

Until it didn't matter any more.

Until the day, one week after Rebecca Walsh and Jenny Cooper had first met, and first clashed, when the bully didn't come to school.

There were whisperings, tiny murmurs of nothing and too little information, but still Jenny tried to listen, still on the outside even when the leader of the enemies was absent. Words caught her attention. *Accident. Hospital. Dead.*

*Accident. Hospital. Dead.*

Three little words. And these three little words settled into Jenny's mind and her imagination took hold of them, held them, hugged them to itself and gave Jenny her answer, the one she had been looking for since she had first ventured into that attic, and which she had been looking for in her dreams (her nightmares) ever since. Rebecca Walsh was gone. And Jenny had a chance to change things. To start fresh. The idea was almost too much, it stole her breath and made her weak. It took the bones from her legs and made her blood pump faster, harder. *It might be all right.*

But then other little words started to fall around her, and although she tried not to hear them, they wormed their way in, giving her doubt, making her wonder. *Recovering. Survived. Lived.*

Jenny didn't like those words.

But the doll, the rag doll with the crooked mouth and the staring, eternally open eyes had told her in her dreams, had visited her and told her over and over that she had done it, that it was starting, that the girl would die.

Jenny had wondered which girl.

Jenny had wondered whether the doll had meant her or the bully. Because someone's death was written for fate to read, and it could have been either of them. But the doll never answered. She just smiled and stared and her silence was maddening and deafening. But Jenny thought that the doll was pleased with her. And that was good.

The wonderings went on until after break time. Then they were told. Mrs Sanderson entered the room, her eyes red and bewildered, her cheeks rubbed dry. The children sat when they saw her, the air full of half-spoken fears and a knowing, too wise feeling. Mrs Sanderson watched them, waited until they were as quiet as they ever would be, and leant against her desk, her arms reaching back behind her, bracing herself for the questions and tears to come. And she looked especially at Jenny, frail, unsure, dark rings under her eyes and a paleness to her face that hadn't been there when she had arrived a week ago. She wondered whether the girl might not be happier now, and then she brushed the thought away, the terrible, uncharitable, yet totally correct thought.

"Now, girls, I have some dreadful news to tell you. And I'm sorry to have to do this. I'm so, so sorry."

The room stirred, it held its breath. It was excited and scared and knew this was a day to remember. Jenny's heart was skipping, staggering, waiting to speed up or slow down as required. Waiting for the news.

"This morning, on the way to school, Rebecca Walsh was involved in a car accident. She was taken to the hospital, and they tried to make her better but ... but we've just heard that Rebecca has died." And the girls watched in awe as they saw a teacher cry for the first time. None of them forgot that. It was something that would come to each of them every now and then, surprising them, until the day they died. They all felt a little more grown up, a little more real.

It took a moment, but other girls started to cry, wailing, sorrowful and deep, pained. Jenny didn't cry. *She broke her neck. She couldn't breathe.* The doll, its voice so quiet she could barely hear it, she had to strain to catch the words. And Jenny, now she knew, wanted everyone to know; "She broke her neck. She couldn't breathe," she said. And then, "It was a bad way to die."

"Jenny!" Mrs Sanderson moved to her side, held her, thinking maybe it was shock, wondering how the girl knew the gruesome details.

And Jenny was quiet. But she smiled. Now it was all right. Now she could live.

They were waiting for her in the attic. In the dark, dark attic. And they knew she was coming, of course. They always knew. They could feel her. It was time to play.

Miss Westerly, head hanging down and heart heavy, slowly climbed the shining spiral staircase. She felt wounded and shaken, she felt too old to be playing with toys, especially in such a deadly game. But some promises, the ones made by nine year olds, could never be broken. They were for keeps.

The attic was as it always was, the toys, abandoned, forgotten except by so few, the tainted, condemned few, playing their eternal game of hangman. The board was ready, only a few letters missing. J _ N N Y C _ _ P _ R. And the man only needed one leg.

Miss Westerly took hold of the chalk and played the game.

# Hunting Shadows

## Mike Brooks

The Goose Fair truly comes alive at night.

For most of the year, the population of Nottingham largely avoid the Forest recreation ground unless it's a very sunny day and they want to do some sunbathing. It's little more than a very long, flat space with a wooded hill on one side, and the neighbourhoods around aren't really anything to write home about. However, for five days at the beginning of October every year, Britain's largest travelling fair rolls up. By day, it doesn't look like much. When darkness falls, it transforms into a riot of noise and light and savoury smells.

The streets around are choked with parked cars and every entrance to the fair has people selling either hot food (always with mushy peas, that truly disgusting speciality that's as much a part of Nottingham as Robin Hood is) or headbands and kids' swords that sparkle with LEDs. The night is pushed back by flashing bulbs and the tinny blast of popular music, and the true ethnic diversity of Nottingham is found inside; people from all backgrounds mixing together around the extortionately-priced rides, eating pies and candy floss and drinking hot drinks, chatting and laughing and screaming in a host of different languages. There are English, Polish, Kurdish, Afghan, Iranian, Indian, Bangladeshi; male and female; young and old.

And, by the coconut shy, a vampire.

I feel it before I see it; a creeping sensation spreading out under my skin from the old bite scar on my neck, like someone pouring cold, greasy dishwater over my flesh. Nothing else I've ever encountered gives me that feeling, and I've seen more weirdness in the Nottingham nights than the average person. Of course, a vampire had a perfect right to be here, blending in and pretending to be human. Hell, I've encountered them in cinemas, late-night pharmacies (although I've never worked out why; do they get ill? Surely they don't need condoms?) and nightclubs, usually minding their own business and never giving a clue to the people around them that *nosferatu* exist outside of Hammer horror movies. Vampires in crowds of people aren't a problem. It's when they're alone with one person, far from help, that you get trouble.

I stop, casually looking around as I lean against one of the pillars of the dodgems. The sensation I get is never directional, but I've learned to pick up a few visual clues. A vampire moves more smoothly than humans and with more assurance, and when they're not moving they stand stiller than any human can ever manage. Especially if they don't remember to keep breathing.

The two kids running back and forth hitting each other with LED swords are out; vampires don't Turn children. The brown-haired woman off to one side clutching a few helium balloons is clearly their mother, so she's out too. A group of guys in their mid-twenties who look to be of Middle Eastern heritage cross my line of vision, chatting and laughing, but I only sense one vamp so it's unlikely to be in their party. The woman talking to the kids' mother? Younger, red-haired, good posture; she's a possibility. I take a couple of casual steps in her direction, but the feeling fades slightly. The vampire's the other way.

I stop and turn, as though I'm trying to work out which ride to go on next. There. Standing right next to a burger van, a large white guy with dark hair pulled back in a tail and a ratty-looking moustache that extends down past his mouth, almost to his chin. Black jeans, black trainers and an Adidas sports jacket that would insulate a human well from the chill of an October night. He stands stock still, nostrils widening slightly as he smells the air, but he's not paying any attention to the meat of dubious origin being fried a few feet from him. His pupils are perhaps slightly larger than usual, a vampire's adaption to night-time hunting. His breath doesn't steam in the air like mine as he exhales before breathing in again, because his body is cool.

He sees me. Only to be expected; word gets around in the vampire community as it does anywhere else, word about the few humans who know that the supernatural is real and will hunt them down if we hear that they've been preying on us. Vampires have got some sort of system going on involving pig blood from farming, they apparently don't *need* human blood at all. It's just that some of them don't want to let go of the past, or else enjoy the thrill of the hunt.

To be fair, it would be easier for me to blend in with the crowd if I didn't have a red mohawk, black-painted nails and a studded leather jacket, but I'm damned if I'm going to change who I am just to hide from a bloody vampire.

He turns and disappears between the burger van and the coconut shy. I follow. If he'd just stood there, stared me out or walked casually away, I wouldn't have thought much of it. Like I said, vampires in a crowd aren't the worry. But this one doesn't want to be seen, which means I want to see him.

Yes, I'm aware it could be a trap, set up by some vampire whose friend I've killed, or maybe just a lunatic who wants to kick off a war. I'm not a total idiot. That's why I never go out unprepared for whatever the night might throw at me, or at least whatever I've already met. You never know what new wonder you might run into, of course, but that's part of the fun. If by 'fun' you mean 'pant-wetting terror'. The two concepts seem inseparable, these days.

He's out of sight, of course, but what he doesn't know is that I can feel his presence. I've been careful never to let that slip to anyone but my friends. He's heading out of the fair, up past the mini-rollercoaster that I've never been on because I simply don't trust something that's been assembled in one afternoon, past the ride that shoots people into the air in a tiny capsule on massive rubber cords like some sort of giant catapult. I see the white diamond of the Adidas logo on the back of his coat as he hurries away up the hill, heading in the direction of the city centre, and I follow him. He seems to be hunting something.

The noise and light are fading behind me now. He's heading into Radford; an odd mix of large Victorian houses and smaller, newer homes for the labourers who worked locally, it's a nest of dark back alleys and narrow streets, drug deals and social deprivation. Maybe not the most sensible place to be following a vampire into, especially not one who knows that I've seen him, but he may not know that I'm following him. Besides, this is my city as much as it is his. I know the ground as well as anyone; probably better in fact, given that I'm a taxi driver when I'm not out protecting the public from things that go bump in the night.

He turns into one of those narrow back alleys, a service road running between the rear gardens of towering Victorian town houses, long ago divided up into flats to maximise the potential rent. Massive, ancient trees reach out overhead, obscuring the night sky with their leaves and casting a thick darkness over the street below that's only intermittently broken by acid yellow illumination from those streetlights that the council have kept in working order. The pavement is cracked and uneven, the road surface is pitted, and I have to step down onto it to go around an old mattress, a burnt-out microwave and other, less recognisable detritus piled outside a back gate. We're already into a world where the city is starting to crumble and the most frequent visitors are drug addicts looking for a secluded shadow to shoot up in.

He slows. I match his pace, placing my feet carefully, keeping close to the crumbling but sturdy wall on my right. Vampire senses are sharper than human ones and he may be able to hear my anyway, but there's no point taking chances. The night air is still, cold and dry, so my scent shouldn't carry. He hasn't looked back, just side to side. I frown. What could he be looking for down this back street that he needs to move stealthily for? Discarded hypodermics and old white cider bottles don't spook easily.

He lunges into the shadow of a gate, a large stone arch slightly set back from the wall it occupies. I hear a grunt of effort from him, and then a thin, tearing scream that can't have come from his frame. He backs out, and I see another form trapped in his grasp, dragged into the partial illumination of the streetlight above my head. Arms and legs visibly scrawny despite the bulkiness of the black material clothing them. Pale, dirty hands and feet. Face hidden in shadow by the hood of a sweatshirt, but dark hair spilling out as it thrashes. Maybe five feet tall, and perhaps half my weight.

He's got a homeless child.

Something flips inside my brain. I don't like children; I find them noisy, messy and generally offensive. But far, far greater than my dislike of kids is my hatred of those that prey on the weak. That child would be lucky to live through the night anyway, given the clear sky and cold night air that promises a heavy frost in an hour or two, and its lack of suitable clothing. It's a crying shame, but that's how things are in cities, and there's nothing I can do about it. Even if I'd known about this kid, there would be others that I didn't know about, that I couldn't help. But a kid snatched out of its pitiful shelter against the elements by a vampire, to be drained of its blood and left for dead; that I *can* do something about.

I don't deal well with anger, over a certain level. I have a tendency to start smashing things. Well, that wasn't necessarily going to be a problem in this situation. This vampire was about to learn why its kind had learned to leave Nottingham's children well alone.

I give a wordless yell and charge. Subtle? No. But in the circumstances, I want the vampire's attention on me as soon as possible. I can look after myself, the kid can't.

The vampire's face turns to me, shock and anger warring for prominence. He didn't know I was behind him, and he's not happy about it. He holds one hand up towards me, palm outstretched in the universal gesture for me to stop. His mouth starts moving but I don't hear the words over my shout. On the far side of his body I see one arm is still wrapped around his victim's neck, and the child's pale fingers are digging in, trying to get free. The vamp's not going to let go, even to deal with me.

I don't slow down as I reach him, just duck under his arm and swing a right hook into his jaw that sends all three of us sprawling to the ground. I hear a muffled hiss of pain from the child, but it's better than having your throat ripped open. I'm more or less on top and I raise my fist to punch the vamp again, but his right arm sweeps up in a back-swing that catches me unprepared and knocks me sprawling into the road.

Vampires hit hard. They aren't the superhuman beings of some legends because you can't change the physics of what a formerly-human body can do, but they are at the pinnacle of human capability. If you imagine a top athlete in peak condition, that's a vampire. And this one was already bigger than me.

Thankfully I'm in pretty good shape myself, and I've got a ridiculously hard head. I sit up with the knowledge that eating is going to be damn painful tomorrow, scramble back to my feet and shout "Run!" at the top of my lungs, in case the kid needed a hint.

There's no kid.

There's a vampire, also getting back to his feet, eyes narrowed in rage and lips curling upwards to reveal his fangs, now fully extended. There's the empty street stretching away on either side of us, towards the open space of the Forest to my right and to where it curves gently around out of sight to my left. There's the wall behind the vampire, possibly eight feet high. But there's no kid.

What the hell?

"Are you blind!?" the vampire snarls, clenching his fists. "This was none of your business!" I can't run. He'd be fast enough to catch me. He's got nothing to lose by talking to me. He's not even wasting breath, since he only needs it to speak.

"The hell it's not," I shoot back, reaching one hand into my jacket pocket. I have a cross in the back pocket of my combats, and if I can shove it into the centre of his chest it can kill him, but I need something to press against. I need him on his back on the ground, or up against a wall, and that won't be easy against someone with his size and strength. "How's your face?"

He reaches one hand up to his cheek, and winces as he encounters two small burn marks. He looks at his fingers, then touches his face again more gingerly. "What...?"

I wave a fist at him, grinning. His eyes focus on the silver rings on my second and fourth fingers. I have iron ones on my index and ring fingers, but iron doesn't hurt vampires. It does hurt some other things though, which is why I have them. Oh, and the studs on the back of my leather jacket? Half of them aren't steel.

"So it *is* you," he growls. "Simon Seys."

He says it 'Simon Says'. I hate it when people do that, it makes me sound like a parlour game.

"It's pronounced 'Sayze'," I correct him. "And yes, it's me. What, the hair's not enough of a distinguishing feature? I've got to tattoo my damn name across my forehead to prevent you idiots from hunting children while I'm around?"

"That wasn't a child," he snarls, taking a step towards me.

"Looked like one to me," I tell him, judging distances.

"Then you're a fool," he spits, "and blind with it." A

nasty smile crosses his face. "I've never hurt a human. You attacked me for no good reason. That puts *you* in breach of the Agreement. That means I get to kill you."

"That means you get to *try*, jackmonkey," I tell him. I want him nearer, but I can only allow him one more step until he gets too close. Vampire fighting is a very fine art, and fine art is hard to do when you're strung out on adrenaline and having images of yourself bleeding out into a gutter. I really need to find less dangerous ways to spend my free time.

He takes the next step. He's got no need to rush into anything; he knows I can't get away from him, but he's cautious because he knows that I've got rings that can hurt him, and if he's got half a brain he knows I must have other tricks that can help me kill his kind. He knows I've done it before.

Still, he doesn't react quickly enough when I pull out a sports bottle of water and squirt a jet into his face. It would be a good blinding tactic anyway, especially since I follow it up by running in and launching a punch at his throat, but it's holy water. It burns his skin on contact and sends up something that might be smoke or might be steam, but is definitely the sign of pain. As is the scream of agony that comes from him.

He covers up, and my punch slides off his arms. I grab him and hook one leg behind his, trying for an *o-soto-gari*, a basic judo throw that will get him on his back and allow me to end this quickly, but he elbows me in the side of the head which knocks me off-balance and sideways, then something like a cannonball hits the right side of my ribcage and I stumble further, nearly tripping over the kerb. I end up leaning against the wall next to the gate he grabbed that kid from — if it was a kid — in the first place.

"I thought you were meant to be tough," he sneers, "one kick to the ribs and you're half dead."

"Better than being all dead," I counter, but he's not far off being right. Needing to breathe is a real handicap when doing so causes most of your right side to flash red-hot in your brain. He's keeping an eye on the bottle I've still got clutched in my left hand. He won't stand still enough for me to splatter him again, especially now there's less in there and I won't be able to squirt it as far, so I take a mouthful. I can spit it at him if I get close.

"You might burn me a bit, but you can't get out of here alive," he tells me flatly. "If you're all there is to worry about, I don't know why more of us don't just hunt you." He starts to approach and I face off with him, right side turned away from him now. I'm right handed, so I prefer my power hand further back anyway, like a boxer. It's just a case of whether or not I can throw anything with it hard enough to give him pause now my ribs are killing me.

He lunges. I spit, knowing it's pointless to try and save it as I need any advantage I can get as soon as I can get it, and a mouthful of water impedes my breathing. I maybe clip an ear; he dodges most of it, and then he's on me before I can swing, bearing me back against the gate with his hands on my upper arms, preventing me from punching or grabbing him. The impact knocks more breath from me, but now I don't have to move my legs to keep from falling over, so I kick him between his.

Yes, testicles still hurt on a vampire. He gives a strangled grunt of pain and bends forward involuntarily, so I head butt him. It takes a moment for my vision to clear, but he's come off worse; his nose looks to be broken, he's bleeding from it and his eyes are slightly glazed. Now it's my turn to lunge at him, trying to tackle him to the ground, but he manages to twist at the last moment and my own forward momentum drives me down onto the gritty tarmac with him following me down. I make a desperate attempt to roll clear, but he gets one knee on my chest to pin me down and he's more than strong enough to hold my arms against the ground.

"Now you've pissed me off," he snarls, face a few inches from mine. I can see the angry red skin where the holy water spattered on him, burning away his skin. I spit at him again just in case there's any left in my mouth, but it does nothing except cause him to knee me in my bad ribs with his other leg. The cross is still trapped in my back pocket, and I'm out of tricks now. What I really need is one of the others to come in and club him in the back of the head, but I'm all alone out here.

All I'd wanted to do this evening was have a bit of fun at the fair.

I can feel him shifting his weight as he licks his newly-extended teeth, making sure I can see it, eyeing up first one side and then the other of my neck. He sniffs deeply, smiling at me ... and suddenly he freezes. I feel his body tense, not with the strain of holding me down but with something deeper. His lips slowly close, his face becoming a blank mask, but nothing else moves. Except his eyes. They dart from side to side, the eyes of a hunted animal.

He's terrified.

He sniffs again, slower, softly, as though trying not to make any noise. His eyes flick up now, looking away above my head, back towards the entrance to this street, towards the distant light and sound of the Goose Fair. Figuring that he's got nothing much to gain by acting, I tilt my head back to try and see what he's looking at.

"*Don't ... move,*" he hisses quietly.

"Sorry, don't mean to disturb your dinner," I say in as close to a normal voice as I can get with a big vampire leaning on my ribs. He shoots me a glare that's nearly enough to kill me in its own right.

"You *are* blind," he mutters. He swallows nervously, which has to be a leftover human reaction. "I'm going to let you up in a second."

"Er … what?" That confused me. Understandably, I feel.

"When I do, run back the way we came," he tells me, lips barely moving. "I'll go the other way. Stay in the middle of the road, and stay out of the shadows."

I frown, completely perplexed. "Why?"

"Because if they have to pick one of us, they might not catch either of us," he says cryptically. Suddenly his knee is gone from my ribs. To my astonishment, I feel him pulling me up by the wrists that a moment ago he was holding pinned against the tarmac. I've barely got my feet under me when he pushes me in the chest, nearly knocking me down again. "Go!"

He turns and runs. I'm too astonished to move, sure that at any moment he's going to turn back and come sprinting after me, some cruel trick to make me think I've got a chance at getting away. But he doesn't. He keeps running.

For about twenty metres, at which point there's suddenly something at his feet that just *wasn't there* a split second ago and he trips, falling to the ground. I'm staring, trying to make sense of what just happened, and then the object rises to its feet.

At first I think it's the child from before. But it's not. It's taller, although still not as tall as me, maybe five feet six, and there's the hint of slightly more heft to the limbs. Mind you, it still looks several meals short of malnutrition, and the face is also hidden in the raised hood of a tracksuit. The hair's different though, long and blonde instead of dark.

Something changes. I couldn't say what, but it seems that I blink, and in the space between my eyes closing and opening again the shadows are occupied. Maybe a dozen figures on either side of me, perched on the high walls and emerging from the dark pools of shade in gateways. All dressed similarly in dark clothes, mainly tracksuits and the like, all with hoods raised, all with faces in shadow. All I see is a faint gleam of reflected light from what might be eyes. And teeth.

The vampire struggles to get away, and it's like his movement triggers a feeding frenzy. There's a sibilant murmur, like wind in the trees if the wind was hungry and sadistic, and the figures leap for the bloodsucker. He's buried under their forms for a moment and I see pale hands rising and falling clutching weapons; a broken bottle, a plank of wood from a fence with the nails still in it, a syringe. Then he's pulled up to his feet and dragged to a streetlight, hands and feet bound to it with thin bits of black plastic; zip ties. One of the attackers grabs his chin and pulls it back and up.

The blonde one that tripped the vampire in the first place walks forward. There's a small *snick* sound, and the blade of a flick knife appears in his hand. The vampire's struggling to get free, but he can't. He's bleeding from half a dozen wounds that I can see, and probably many more than I can't. He's trying to scream or shout, but with his mouth clamped shut it's coming out muffled. Nonetheless, he's making enough noise that sooner or later someone might come and see what's going on.

The blonde figure places his blade almost lovingly against the base of the vampire's throat. I want to look away, but I don't dare. I want to see what's happening, to judge when I can get the hell out of here. That doesn't mean I'm prepared to see the blonde figure punch the knife into the vampire's flesh and perform a simple, brutal but effective tracheotomy.

My stomach churns and I struggle to hold on to my dinner. It's self-preservation that helps me, in the end. I don't want to do anything that might draw attention to myself. The vampire is trying to scream, but the air's just whistling out of the gaping hole in his throat. He won't be making enough noise to bring anyone running now, however long he tries. He might have to try for a long time. Sure, he's bleeding, but you're going to have to do a lot more than that to finally lay a vampire to rest. They can take damage that would kill a human. Suddenly, that looks like being a bad thing for him.

They start to slice his clothing off him with the same expert ease that a professional chef might use to peel an onion. Then they start on his skin, with what sounds like whispered glee bouncing back and forth amongst them.

It's too much. They seem occupied, and I can't watch any more of this. Whether or not my movement will spur them to attack, I have to try and get out of here. So I turn to run, and find my way blocked by the creature that I'd originally taken to be a child. Somehow, despite no distinguishing features, I recognise it.

"Halt, mortal," it whispers in a thrumming hiss, odd harmonics bouncing around its voice. I pull up short, uncertain of what to do.

"Why do you run?" the creature asks, head tilting to one side. Its speech sounds stilted, as though it is speaking an unfamiliar language. Which it almost certainly is.

"I think I left the gas on," I hear my voice say. Way to go,

Simon. A wisecrack *and* a cultural reference this thing almost certainly won't understand? You sure know how to make friends.

"Why did you come to my aid?" the creature asks. I notice that the light from the pole where the vampire is being ... whatever ... is behind me. I should be able to see into the hood, should be able to see this thing's face, but I can't. It's still hidden in darkness, and that both reassures and unnerves me at the same time. I realise that I've been asked another question, and panic as I try to find an answer.

"I thought you were a child," I say, then curse myself. Mistaken identity. Yes, I'm really going to piss this thing off.

"You care for the young of your species?" it hisses curiously.

"Not as a rule," I shrug. Answering the last one honestly didn't get me killed, may as well stick with it. The creature tilts its head again, and I get the impression that I'm being regarded intently from inside that dark hood.

"You are interesting, mortal," it hisses after a few seconds which seem to last about three hundred years. Then it nods its head to me slightly. "I thank you for my life. I was careless. The drinker would have taken me."

"Don't mention it," I say, nonplussed. There is something really, really odd about having this polite conversation while the vampire in question is being tortured to death behind me.

"If you insist," the creature says, and makes a motion with one hand towards its mouth. I realise it took my statement literally. Note to self: avoid expressions like 'well, bugger me' when talking to it.

It stands to one side, removing itself from my path. "Go,

mortal. Your gas is waiting."

"Uh ... okay. Thanks." I take a step, unable to believe my luck. But yes, I guess I did save this thing's life. Some debts of gratitude will still be honoured, no matter how depraved the creatures involved. I find my mouth moving without my brain's intervention once more. "Wait."

Its hood turns towards me again.

"What are you?" I gesture around, trying to express with a gesture my confusion at its companions emerging from apparent thin air. "A shadow?"

"'Shadow' is a good name," the thing hisses in what I take to be amusement, "but no, mortal, we are not shadows. We are aelfar."

It prowls off towards the others, like a cat if it walked on its hind legs and was really, seriously creepy. I watch it until my eyes fall on the red ruin of the vampire, still twitching and thrashing as the aelfar have their fun. Then I turn, set my eyes on the end of the road and start walking, firmly and quickly. There are far worse things than vampires haunting the shadows of the cities.

The elves are still here.

# THE DEAD GIRL

### GUY DE MAUPASSANT

I had loved her madly!

Why does one love? Why does one love? How queer it is to see only one being in the world, to have only one thought in one's mind, only one desire in the heart, and only one name on the lips — a name which comes up continually, rising, like the water in a spring, from the depths of the soul to the lips, a name which one repeats over and over again, which one whispers ceaselessly, everywhere, like a prayer.

I am going to tell you our story, for love only has one, which is always the same. I met her and loved her; that is all. And for a whole year I have lived on her tenderness, on her caresses, in her arms, in her dresses, on her words, so completely wrapped up, bound, and absorbed in everything which came from her, that I no longer cared whether it was day or night, or whether I was dead or alive, on this old earth of ours.

And then she died. How? I do not know; I no longer know anything. But one evening she came home wet, for it was raining heavily, and the next day she coughed, and she coughed for about a week, and took to her bed. What

119

happened I do not remember now, but doctors came, wrote, and went away. Medicines were brought, and some women made her drink them. Her hands were hot, her forehead was burning, and her eyes bright and sad. When I spoke to her, she answered me, but I do not remember what we said. I have forgotten everything, everything, everything! She died, and I very well remember her slight, feeble sigh. The nurse said, "Ah!" and I understood, I understood!

I knew nothing more, nothing. I saw a priest, who said, "Your mistress?" and it seemed to me as if he were insulting her. As she was dead, nobody had the right to say that any longer, and I turned him out. Another came who was very kind and tender, and I shed tears when he spoke to me about her.

They consulted me about the funeral, but I do not remember anything that they said, though I recollected the coffin, and the sound of the hammer when they nailed her down in it. Oh! God, God!

She was buried! Buried! She! In that hole! Some people came — female friends. I made my escape and ran away. I ran, and then walked through the streets, went home, and the next day started on a journey.

Yesterday I returned to Paris, and when I saw my room again — our room, our bed, our furniture, everything that remains of the life of a human being after death — I was seized by such a violent attack of fresh grief, that I felt like opening the window and throwing myself out into the street. I could not remain any longer among these things, between these walls which had enclosed and sheltered her, which retained a thousand atoms of her, of her skin and of her breath, in their imperceptible crevices. I took up my hat to make my escape, and just as I reached the door, I passed the large glass in the hall, which she had put there so that she might look at herself every day from head to foot as she went out, to see if her toilette looked well, and was correct and pretty, from her little boots to her bonnet.

I stopped short in front of that looking-glass in which she had so often been reflected — so often, so often, that it must have retained her reflection. I was standing there, trembling, with my eyes fixed on the glass — on that flat, profound, empty glass — which had contained her entirely, and had possessed her as much as I, as my passionate looks had. I felt as if I loved that glass. I touched it; it was cold. Oh! The recollection! Sorrowful mirror, burning mirror, horrible mirror, to make men suffer such torments! Happy is the man whose heart forgets everything that it has contained, everything that has passed before it, everything that has looked at itself in it, or has been reflected in its affection, in its love! How I suffer!

I went out without knowing it, without wishing it, and toward the cemetery. I found her simple grave, a white marble cross, with these few words:

*She loved, was loved, and died.*

She is there, below, decayed! How horrible! I sobbed with my forehead on the ground, and I stopped there for a long time, a long time. Then I saw that it was getting dark, and a strange, mad wish, the wish of a despairing lover, seized me. I wished to pass the night, the last night, in weeping on her grave. But I should be seen and driven out. How was I to manage? I was cunning, and got up and began to roam about in that city of the dead. I walked and walked. How small this city is, in comparison with the other, the city in which we live. And yet, how much more numerous the dead are than the living. We want high houses, wide streets, and much room for the four generations who see the daylight at the same time, drink water from the spring, and wine from the vines, and eat bread from the plains.

And for all the generations of the dead, for all that ladder of humanity that has descended down to us, there is scarcely anything, scarcely anything! The earth takes them back, and oblivion effaces them. Adieu!

At the end of the cemetery, I suddenly perceived that I was in its oldest part, where those who had been dead a long time are mingling with the soil, where the crosses themselves are decayed, where possibly newcomers will be put tomorrow. It is full of untended roses, of strong and dark cypress-trees, a sad and beautiful garden, nourished on human flesh.

I was alone, perfectly alone. So I crouched in a green tree and hid myself there completely amid the thick and sombre branches. I waited, clinging to the stem, like a shipwrecked man does to a plank.

When it was quite dark, I left my refuge and began to walk softly, slowly, inaudibly, through that ground full of dead people. I wandered about for a long time, but could not find her tomb again. I went on with extended arms, knocking against the tombs with my hands, my feet, my knees, my chest, even with my head, without being able to find her. I groped about like a blind man finding his way; I felt the stones, the crosses, the iron railings, the metal wreaths, and the wreaths of faded flowers! I read the names with my fingers, by passing them over the letters. What a night! What a night! I could not find her again!

There was no moon. What a night! I was frightened, horribly frightened in these narrow paths, between two rows of graves. Graves! Graves! Graves! Nothing but graves! On my right, on my left, in front of me, around me, everywhere there were graves! I sat down on one of them, for I could not walk any longer, my knees were so weak. I could hear my heart beat! And I heard something else as well. What? A confused, nameless noise. Was the noise in my head, in the impenetrable night, or beneath the mysterious earth, the earth sown with human corpses? I looked all around me, but I cannot say how long I remained there; I was paralysed with terror, cold with fright, ready to shout out, ready to die.

Suddenly, it seemed to me that the slab of marble on which I was sitting, was moving. Certainly it was moving, as if it were being raised. With a bound, I sprang on to the neighbouring tomb, and I saw, yes, I distinctly saw the stone which I had just quitted rise upright. Then the dead person appeared, a naked skeleton, pushing the stone back with its bent back. I saw it quite clearly, although the night was so dark. On the cross I could read:

*Here lies Jacques Olivant, who died at the age of fifty-one. He loved his family, was kind and honourable, and died in the grace of the Lord.*

The dead man also read what was inscribed on his tombstone; then he picked up a stone off the path, a little, pointed stone and began to scrape the letters carefully. He slowly effaced them, and with the hollows of his eyes he looked at the places where they had been engraved. Then with the tip of the bone that had been his forefinger, he wrote in luminous letters, like those lines which boys trace on walls with the tip of a Lucifer match:

*Here reposes Jacques Olivant, who died at the age of*

*fifty-one. He hastened his father's death by his unkindness, as he wished to inherit his fortune, he tortured his wife, tormented his children, deceived his neighbours, robbed everyone he could, and died wretched.*

When he had finished writing, the dead man stood motionless, looking at his work. On turning round I saw that all the graves were open, that all the dead bodies had emerged from them, and that all had effaced the lies inscribed on the gravestones by their relations, substituting the truth instead. And I saw that all had been the tormentors of their neighbours — malicious, dishonest, hypocrites, liars, rogues, calumniators, envious; that they had stolen, deceived, performed every disgraceful, every abominable action, these good fathers, these faithful wives, these devoted sons, these chaste daughters, these honest tradesmen, these men and women who were called irreproachable. They were all writing at the same time, on the threshold of their eternal abode, the truth, the terrible and the holy truth of which everybody was ignorant, or pretended to be ignorant, while they were alive.

I thought that *she* also must have written something on her tombstone, and now running without any fear among the half-open coffins, among the corpses and skeletons, I went toward her, sure that I should find her immediately. I recognised her at once, without seeing her face, which was covered by the winding-sheet, and on the marble cross, where shortly before I had read:

*She loved, was loved, and died.*

I now saw:

*Having gone out in the rain one day, in order to deceive her lover, she caught cold and died.*

It appears that they found me at daybreak, lying on the grave unconscious.

# NIGHT TERRORS

# LAST NIGHT IN BILOXI

## ROBERT J. MENDENHALL

Horner slammed the wooden door behind him and fell against it, his back and arms bracing it, reinforcing it, pleading with it to be strong enough.

Please, be strong enough.

His mouth opened and closed like a suffocating fish. His heart rifled into his chest. Sweat stung his wide eyes. It was dark in the room. Coal mine dark and he could see nothing but the after-image of those burning, fire-yellow eyes.

He cocked his head to the side, resting his ear on the old door, listening through the scratchy wood to the other side. But he could only hear the raspy push and pull of his laboured breathing. He clamped his jaw and screwed his eyes shut, willing his heart to slow and his lungs to function properly. He exhaled long and slow, and then took a deep pull of air through his nose.

The stench assailed him at once and he covered mouth and nose with his hand. The rotting odour of human faeces, old and recent, baking in the Mississippi heat, drove him to nausea. He slid partially down the door. Bile backwashed into his throat. He choked it down and pushed himself back up and against the door.

He rolled his body, pressing his shoulder to the door now, pressing the door deep into its jamb. There had to be a lock. He felt along the side of the door for the knob. Had to be. He had to find it before that thing got here. He had to lock the god-damn door.

There. The door knob. He grasped it with his free hand, feeling along the warm, slick bulb with his thumb. It was smooth. No lock. He pushed and pulled on the knob. No lock.

Shit.

He heard the scraping outside. Like claws dragged over gravel. His breath skipped.

He slid his hand up along the woodwork, along the door frame, back over the door.

The scraping grew louder. Closer.

His fingers brushed over the bolt.

The scraping stopped.

He fumbled in the dark with the bolt, his hands shaking so badly he could barely feel the metal. He grasped the arm of the bolt, worked it free, and slid the bolt across the frame into its mate.

The door exploded against him and he cried out as he fell hard to the sticky floor. He turned over, expecting to see those fiery eyes lumbering over him, feel hot saliva dripping onto him from a gaping, rancid mouth. But the door was still intact. It must be. He could barely see it.

Another crash and it looked as if the door had shaken in its frame. He scampered backwards on heels and hands and careened into the wall, his fingers sliding through something moist.

Another crash.

And another.

He gathered his legs into his chest, pulling himself into

a tight bundle, his back against the hard surface of the wall.

He waited for the next blow.

His pumping blood roared in his ears. Sweat beaded on his temples and ran down his cheeks, pasting thin, walnut hair to his forehead.

But nothing came. Had it gone? Had it left?

Minutes eased by. Long minutes that could have been hours, they seemed so empty. He could hear nothing on the other side of the door — not a sound of night, not a sound of anything. He leaned his head against the wall and trembled, his body aching and exhausted at the intensity of its own reactions.

He lifted his hand to wipe sweat from his brow and winced at the sudden odour. His hand had slid through something foul and he knew what it was. His nostrils flaring, he wiped his palm on the wall.

Overhead, high on the wall above him, a hint of light diffused through a tiny, glazed-over window. He hadn't noticed it before, but no surprise there. The moon must have risen since and the weak glow through the glazing cast a whisper of shadow into the small room. He blew out a breath of exasperation.

A men's room.

He had taken refuge in a fucking toilet.

The cramped room made him claustrophobic in the dark. He could make out the stained urinal only inches from his face and now that he knew it was there, its acidic stench punched him. He turned away and saw the tiny stall, its rusty door askew and consumed with graffiti. The toilet had backed up and overflowed and layers of shit and watered-down urine spilled onto the chipped, tile floor. Some of it had been there a while. Some looked recent. The single-bowl porcelain sink was crusty with mineral deposits, the pipes beneath it embossed with rust.

He turned away in disgust and remembered the filth on his hand. He could taste the bile in his throat again.

It was silent out there. Not a sound. Not even the singing of crickets. Had it gone? Had it moved onto find some other prey?

Slowly he pushed himself to his feet. He kept his back tight to the wall, feeling the crisp edges of chipped paint right through the sweat-soaked material of his shirt. He stared at the door in the dim light. It could be out there waiting for him. Waiting for him to pull back the bolt, to ease open the door, to peer out...

Waiting for him.

Jesus, why him? Why was this happening? But he knew why. Shit, he knew exactly why. It was his last night in Biloxi, so why the hell hadn't he left that crazy old fuck alone? And why the hell didn't he stay with the others?

He stared at the door in the dull light. The edges were chipped and ragged and paint peeled from its back like it did the walls. Rusty screws secured the thick bolt to the door and—

The room went dark.

He flattened against the wall as his heart lurched. Something was outside the window. Blocking the moonlight. Looking in?

Something scratched at the glass; he could hear it like nails on a blackboard. His chest rose and fell, rose and fell, rose and fell...

Scratching. Trying to get in. Scratching.

Then, silence. Long moments of nothing.

A soft rustle at the glass and the light was back. No brighter than it had been, but nearly blinding in its return.

He closed his eyes against it, against the room, against the vision of whatever it was that was out there.

He wiped his brow with the back of his clean hand, and took long pulls of the putrid air, his ribs aching, his stomach seething.

The old man had done this. That old black coot had sent this ... this thing for him.

It's funny how in Biloxi, right along the strip, you can have these bright high-rolling, high-energy, casinos with their big name entertainment and all-you-can-eat buffets and on the other side, literally right across the street, these dilapidated, low-to-no income shacks infested with poverty and rodents. Right across the street. It was so fucking funny.

They should have just left him alone. It was their last night in town. They should have just walked on by. They had laughed at the old man, the three of them had. Rick, Alex, and Horner.

Why had they even crossed the street? His car was in the parking deck on the strip.

The old man was just rocking in his old wicker chair, chewing on something, spitting over the porch rail. What had he found so funny in that? The booze had worked its way into his system and he had won a few hundred at the casino, so he was pretty wired. It hadn't taken much. The old man spat and they laughed. The old man rocked and they laughed. The old man cussed at them and they stopped laughing.

"What did you say?" Horner asked the old man.

"Nuttin'" The old man's words were thick as his tongue slid over toothless gums.

"Bullshit." Horner was incensed. "What the fuck did you say to me?" He stomped over the patchy lawn. The old man stopped his rocking.

"I say nuttin to you."

Horner reached over the porch rail and grabbed the old man by his tobacco stained tee shirt. He pulled him from the rocker and twisted the shirt into his fist. The old man's bony arms lay flaccid at his sides, his thin neck held his leathery head askew. The old man's breath stank of garlic and his eyes were mustard-coloured and deep. His lips were cracked at the corners, shiny with tobacco juice.

"I said, what did you say to me?"

"I say nuttin to you."

Horner balled his free fist and held it level with the old man's eyes. "Hey, Mark," Alex said to Horner. "Back off. He's just an old man."

"Yeah, forget about it," said Rick. "You don't want him to voo-doo you, now do ya?" The two laughed out loud. Horner sneered.

Horner stared into the old man's jaundiced eyes. They stared back. Evenly. Directly. Clearly. Horner lowered his fist and released the old man's shirt. He jabbed a finger toward the old man's face, held it for a second, then turned and walked off.

"I'm heading back to the hotel," Horner said to the others.

"Screw that, I'm going back to the casino," said Rick.

"Yeah, me too. I feel lucky," said Alex.

"Well, screw you both," Horner told them. Alex and Rick turned back toward the strip and Horner turned the other way. He looked back over his shoulder and saw the old man standing on his porch looking directly at him. The old man spat over the rail and continued to watch as Horner ambled off into the dark.

Horner heard the scraping again, from outside the door. And a low, throaty growl. What the hell was it? What had that old man sent after him? The scraping stopped abruptly and he felt his scalp rise. His eyes focused on the back of the door. He stared at it, tried to stare through it, tried to—

He jumped at the crash, turning his shoulder into the wall, reaching high along the wall as if he could climb over it.

Another crash. And another. He shot a glance over his shoulder at the door, only feet away. It still stood, but each impact caused it to shake on its hinges.

Another.

And now, between blows, an animal grunt of exertion. With each blow the grunt became more guttural, more intense.

Horner closed his eyes. He screwed them tight and turned his face into the wall. Chips of flaky paint scratched his cheeks. The pounding persisted and grew more fierce. The grunts became deep, animal growls of fury. He slapped his hands over his ears, no longer caring about the filth. His lungs burned.

And, yet again, the pounding stopped.

Outside the door, a low growl tapered off into silence.

Horner freed his ears and rested a forearm between the wall and his forehead. He leaned into it, his throat tight, his face wet, his clothing soaked with the sweat of fear. He could smell his own fear. It overpowered the stink of shit and piss that permeated the filthy little men's room in this filthy shit-box of a whatever it was. And he realised he had no idea where he was.

He could see the blue and red neon of his hotel from the old man's front lawn. It was off the strip, but not far, just down the I-110 spur to Interstate 10. You could get to it by car off the 110, but on foot, from where he was, you needed to walk through one of the most economically depressed areas of Biloxi.

It was late and dark and the streets reeked of chicory and gumbo. And it was stone quiet. While the strip was bright and loud and alive, two blocks north it was a tomb. Not one car drove past him. Not one person was on the street. Horner heard his own footsteps echo in the distance.

The night air was sticky with humidity. The moon was just rising. He pulled his tie from his neck, folded it carefully, and tucked it into the pocket of his sports coat. He continued walking toward the neon beacon, his footfalls the only sound.

Twice he glanced back and both times the old man was standing on his porch, watching Horner walk away. The third time, though, the old man was gone.

Horner stopped and stared at the old man's shack far down the block he had just come. The porch was empty, but so what? The old coot just went inside, right?

Sure, that was it. He took off his sports coat and

gathered it in his hand. His shirt was damp.

Horner turned back in the direction of his hotel and continued. The street terminated in a T and he angled left, the same general direction of the hotel. The streets grew darker, the aroma less apparent. Here the buildings were scattered and few. The lots were large and open and probably at one time bore shacks like the old black man's.

But not now. Now they were empty and dark. Ahead, near the ramp of the 110, at the end of a gravel lot, stood a white, box-framed structure with a single-sided roof.

Overhead on the 110, he could hear the sporadic rush of cars. And the crickets. He hadn't paid any attention to them before, they were lost in the background noise. But he noticed them now, because they had just that moment gone silent. Horner stopped, looked around, and then spun around. He could hear the occasional car drive along the spur, but nothing else.

He had another six or seven blocks through dark streets to get to his hotel. The best way would be—

It was a bark like he had never heard before. No dog could have made it. It was a short and clipped and dripping and when Horner glanced in the direction it came from, he froze. He could only see the silhouette in the dark. The body was massive and lumbered straight toward him on thick shadows of legs. *Two legs.* A deep rumble emanated from it, like a low, persistent growl. Its arms swayed as it moved and, *oh Jesus*, it was going to get him.

Horner stood immobile, fixed on the thing's approach. It drew closer to him, eclipsing the beat-up shacks on the street behind it. He couldn't move. The musky stink of a wet dog hung in the breeze. The growl deepened. Twin slits of yellow blazed high on the shadowed head.

Horner back-stepped, his feet rolling over stones, his

eyes fixed on the glowing yellow slits. Watching them narrow. He pivoted and stumbled as he changed direction, dropping his coat as he pushed off the gravel.

He ran toward the white building with the single angled roof. Behind him, the erratic footfalls stopped and Horner cocked his head over his shoulder as he ran. The thing had snatched his coat from the ground, brought it to its snout, and then started after him again.

Horner reached the side of the building, his chest heaving. He raced around the back, past a metal roll-off dumpster strewn with trash and discarded auto parts. There. At the corner — a door...

*You don't want him to voo-doo you, now do ya?*

The old fucker *had* voo-dooed him or something like it. Horner was sure of it. The old man had summoned some sort of beast.

The tiny window exploded inward. Horner covered his face as shards of glass rained down. The beast bellowed deeply. A fur-covered articulated arm reached through the small opening and groped along the wall, slapping the surface in search. The reek of wet-fur reached him as Horner dodged the limb and bumped his way to the other side of the room.

The light was completely cut off as the creature obscured the window, fumbling blindly for him. Horner crashed into the door, the bolt bruising his shoulder.

Was this his chance? While the creature was on the other side? Could he throw back the bolt and run and get far enough away before the thing started after him? It wasn't fast, was it? No. He didn't think it was fast. Otherwise it would have caught him before he had made it in here.

He glanced to where the window should be. No light. He heard the slapping of its hand on the wall, the incessant rumble of its growl.

Horner patted the dark wall until he felt the bolt. He threw it back and froze. Suddenly there was silence and he could see his hand on the bolt.

He threw the bolt back into place just as the door rocked with the creature's blows. Between each blow, he heard the rising, dripping growl. Horner backed away from the door and lowered himself to the floor, leaning against the corner between the urinal and the sink, his eyes fixed on the door.

The pounding went on and on and on.

He lowered his head to his knees. The sobs started slowly, and then overtook him. Tears mixed with sweat as his chest heaved.

"Fuck it," he spat. "Fuck it." He raised his head from his knees and shouted "Leave me alone! Leave me alone! P-please … please."

And the pounding stopped.

Horner sat with his back wedged in the corner and waited for it to begin again. He waited and the minutes dragged into an hour. He could hear crickets, now, outside in the distance.

A soft knock rapped on the door startling him. He pushed himself to his feet slowly, his eyes fixed on the door.

Again, the soft knocking. Rap … Rap … Rap…

And then a voice.

"You's in dere, Misser? You's okay?"

Horner's body nearly slumped back to the floor. A rush

of relief chilled him. It was the old man. Horner got up and made for the door.

Voo doo, my ass.

"Yeah," Horner said, throwing back the bolt. He opened the door and, standing there in the door way was the old man, all right, with his tobacco stained tee-shirt and gaunt arms and mustard-eyes and everything.

"You's okay?" the old man asked again. "You's lookin' kinda spooked."

So that was it. He had wanted to scare the shit out of Horner. To pay Horner back for rousting him like that. The old coot must have had one of his low-rent cousins dress up like a fucking werewolf or something. Yeah. Still, he looked over the old man's head, peering out into the dark night.

Nothing. That was it. The old man wanted to scare him. Horner took a deep breath of night air. "Yeah, I'm fine," he said as he pushed past him.

"Okay, sure. But I think, maybe, you's dropped dis."

Horner stopped and turned back. The old man raised his hand. He held out Horner's sports coat. Horner looked at it with annoyance, and reached to snatch it from the old man when the odour of wet fur touched him. He looked up at the old man.

Into mustard-eyes that brightened into narrow, fiery slits.

The crickets stopped and Horner wished to God he had left Biloxi the night before.

# LIKE FATHER LIKE DAUGHTER

ROBERT ESSIG

*Mummy, daddy wants to see you again.*

Gale stared out the window, her daughter's voice chattering in her mind as the little girl stared up from the front yard, yellow hair blowing with the wind. Her eyes had been beautiful ... once.

*He'll be back, Mummy, really he will. You'll see.*

"Leave me alone," whispered Gale, eyes red from lack of sleep, frustration, tears, and madness.

She didn't know how it happened, how her husband hid his secret from her for so many years, how they had a child together with such a perilous lie between them — well, not so much between them as within *him*; a secret life.

He had called it a secret, but she knew better. It was no secret. It was a bald-faced lie, the kind of lie that breaks up families, the kind of lie that leads to...

*Mummy, don't be so sad.*

She stared up from the front yard, hands clasped together at her waist, blue dress and stockings — just a little girl who should never have been brought into this world, not with her father's blood. His very being damned her.

139

They named her Greta-Marie, after both of her grandmothers. It was truly the best day of Gale's life when her daughter was born, but it turned out to be a curse, and she knew damn well where her husband, Randolph, had been all those nights when she woke in the hospital to check on the baby only to find that he was gone — not in the bathroom, or the lobby, or at the cafeteria like he had told her.

Now Greta stood at his grave, if that's what it could be called. After Gale killed him and dismembered his body she dragged his remains outside and buried him beneath the walkway, that way the ground would become hardened beneath her feet as she walked to the house ensuring that he could never get out, though she didn't think he really *could* get out after being chopped to pieces, did she?

Well, his daughter — Gale refused to call the little girl *hers* — stood there, taunting her with that uncanny ability to speak in her mind, smiling bright enough to showcase her teeth, especially the sharp incisors.

How could Randolph had hid his vampirism? How could he live so carefully as not to reveal his secret and hope to live a normal life? Well, he tried. He claimed to have had a skin condition that left him perilous to sunlight, restricting him indoors during the day, napping. She worked the graveyard shift, so his problem with the sun worked in his favour since she slept during the day as well.

It was too perfect, and nothing was like the movies. He loved garlic, and crosses couldn't burn an X on his head unless it was branding iron hot.

Gale wept. She couldn't believe her stupidity, her ignorance, but there was more to it. He had abilities, manipulations that he worked on her mind. There could be no other explanation as to how they could have lived for so many years without her discovering his vampirism.

*Okay Mummy, here I go,* Greta said in Gale's mind.

Gale's lip trembled as she looked out of the window at her daughter crouched on the ground, on her knees, digging with her hands in the soft soil where her father's body was buried, the walkway not tread enough after his demise as to create a thick dirt crust.

"Don't do that!" screamed Gale. She opened the window and screamed to his daughter again, "Don't do that! What are you doing?"

"Daddy's coming back, Mummy, you'll see." Her delicate little voice drifted through the still night. At one time Gale loved Greta's voice, relished when her daughter learned how to say "mummy", but now she loathed it.

*Even if she digs him up,* thought Gale, *he'll never come back. After what I did to him, there's no way he can come back.*

The dominoes had fallen over time. Gale had begun to notice something about her daughter that wasn't quite right, and Randolph refused to allow Greta to see a doctor. One day Gale grabbed her daughter's hand and was given a chill at how cold the little girl's skin was. Greta was thin and deathly pale, and she was very sick. Gale persisted that she see a doctor, but Randolph again refused, vehemently. "I've got her," he said. "You just go to work and let *me* take care of her."

That day, Gale had left for work against her better judgment. On her lunch break she had decided to take the rest of the day off and returned home to check on her little girl. What she saw when she came home turned her stomach. Even now she had a difficult time registering the carnage, the gruesomeness of what they were doing to that poor woman. She was still alive, struggling beneath

Randolph's grip as Greta-Marie gluttonously drank from the woman's bleeding wrist. The little girl smiled as blood soiled her dress, wetting her pale face in deep crimson. Then Randolph thrust his face to the woman's neck and ripped out her throat like a savage beast, creating a geyser of blood father and daughter partook of in some twisted family ritual Gale could never understand.

Gale saw this all from the picture window at the front of the house, appalled and shocked. There was an axe leaning against the siding from Randolph's efforts at chopping cords wood for the coming winter. She grabbed it without hesitation.

The door swung open revealing the bloody mess that was her husband and daughter, both of them laughing and slurping from the woman's ruined neck that was finally ceasing its geyser-like spray in the wake of her death.

Randolph stood, a look on his face like he was caught in bed with another woman, which, consequently, would have been better than sharing a cannibalistic feast with their daughter.

Gale took the axe to his head bringing him down with a force she didn't think she was capable of. Her fury took over as she hacked him up. The blood coursing through his veins — what he had sucked from the woman lying dead of the arterial tear in her throat — splattered the walls and ceiling as she flung the axe cutting his appendages from his torso.

Greta ran and hid, and Gale wasn't sure she could have killed her daughter had she the chance. Now she watched as that wretched thing dug her father's body parts from the earth, arranging them neatly in a row: a foot, a leg, a bicep, a hand.

Gale sat and watched, wondering if she could do what

she knew she had to: kill Greta-Marie. It had to be done. The little girl was a beast, a creature of the night, something vile that feasted on human blood. Not her daughter, not the little girl who enjoyed bath time and puzzles. No, that heathen was *his.*

*How could it happen?* thought Gale. Her life was so good and it seemed like just yesterday she was playing patty-cake with Greta, laughing and watching cartoons. Why did Randolph attempt to marry and be happy like a normal person? Why did he do this to Gale?

*Almost done, Mummy! Daddy's coming back!*

"Shut up! Stop talking in my head!"

Gale wept.

Greta giggles in Gale's mind. The little girl hasn't harnessed her abilities yet, can't manipulate the way her father had manipulated her mother so often in the past. She just talks to mummy without opening her mouth, excited that she is going to bring daddy back, the memory of what happened, the rage her mother lashed out on her father with, something that has faded from her memory even though it was only a few days ago that mummy killed him.

Greta has to save daddy, she can't survive without him, and she's getting hungry. Daddy knows the right place to bite to get to the food.

Her tiny hands dig through the dirt, feeling for pieces of daddy. She doesn't quite understand why mummy did what she did, but she supposes it is something mummies do to daddies.

Another foot emerges, of which she places neatly in the row of daddy's anatomy. She notices a spade shovel leaning against the white picket fence and decides to try and use it to dig the rest of daddy out, but she's too little and can't keep her balance.

Her digging becomes more furious, and then she uncovers something round and her face lights up with a smile that reveals her glinting vampire teeth. "Daddy! It's you!"

His eyes are caked with moist dirt as are his nose and ears, but his mouth is closed, and as his daughter attempts to scrape the dirt away from the orifices, it opens, taking a wheezing breath, choking on the dirt that has caked to the severed mess Gale made of his neck, the arteries and tendons hanging there like wires from the back of a stolen car radio.

As daddy's head begins to understand, to remember, to assess reality, his other pieces begin to undulate; toes wriggling on a foot; fingers grasping on a hand; muscles twitching on a leg.

A scream issues from the house.

Gale couldn't believe what she was seeing. The body parts began moving like individual entities after Randolph's head was exhumed. They looked like malformed animals or toys.

"No," she whispered. "He can't come back."

*Of course he's coming back, Mummy. We're going to be together again.*

Then Greta uncovered the torso, pulling it grudgingly

from the loose soil along with the other foot and other arm. The child giggled as she arranged her father's body parts like some morbid puzzle. She'd always liked puzzles, hadn't she?

Gale watched, tears blurring her vision of the macabre ritual taking place in front of her house. The little girl she once cared for, deranged, playing with her father's dismembered corpse, but was he indeed dead? The pieces, however irrational, were moving amongst themselves.

The front door and the windows were locked, Gale was sure of it. They couldn't get in. Even if he does…

Then it began. The pieces fused themselves back onto Randolph's torso. He was dirty, naked and forlorn, grovelling in the soil as he began his re-awakening.

*Yes, Daddy,* said Greta's little voice in Gail's mind.

Then his little girl went to the front door and opened it.

Gale gasped. She could swear she locked the door after burying his body, locked it for fear that his daughter would try to corrupt her.

Gale raced downstairs fearing what she would meet down there. Greta crossed the floor with a bundle of clothing in her arms. The little girl caught a glimpse of her mother and turned her head, face smeared with dirt, grinning a display of sharp teeth.

"Daddy needs clothes, then we'll be together again! Isn't that great, Mummy?" Greta's excitement was numbing.

Gale didn't have the heart to kill her. It was as if the little girl had no idea of what she was, that her existence was a scar on the face of humanity, that her life could not be sustained without the shed of innocent blood.

Greta returned outside with the clothes. Gale was at the door instantly, locking it in her daughter's wake. If she could help it, they weren't coming back inside.

Gale waited. The room was quite rank from the vile display her daughter and husband had made of that woman's body two days ago. Though Gale tried to clean the mess up, the blood had stained the hardwood floor, and she was in too fragile a state to try and re-paint the walls and ceiling.

Gale's weary eyes stared at the front door waiting for them to knock. *How long would it be before they left her alone?* she wondered.

From the door came a rattling.

They were trying to get in.

But the rattling wasn't the doorknob — no, it was the deadbolt, and to Gale's surprise, it slid out of the lock as if they had a key, and it occurred to her just then that Greta must have taken a key out with the clothes.

As the door opened, wind flickered the flames of the kerosene lamps Gale had been using to light the downstairs after Randolph and Greta's blasphemous act. She couldn't bare the room to be lit very brightly, didn't want to see the bloodstains.

"My dear," said Randolph mischievously showcasing his bright fangs with a gleaming smile. His face was smeared and crusted with dirt, as were his hands. "Oh, the things you do to me."

"Stay away from me, Randolph. I'm warning you!"

"Warning me? Really? *You're* going to warn *me*?"

"I'll kill you again, I swear it."

"I don't think so."

Randolph advanced quite rapidly and swept his wife into his arms. "It's been days since we've eaten, darling, and we're famished." He bared his fangs, eyes wide, enveloping his next meal.

"But Daddy," Greta interrupted. "Aren't you going to

make her like we are?"

He paused. "Of course, young one."

Gale squirmed in his grasp, but he was far too powerful. His teeth sunk into her neck with something close to passion. He was delicate but it still hurt, and once the holes were punctured, he moaned as he sucked the life from her.

Greta doesn't know anything about vampirism, doesn't know why they drink blood, why the sun hurts her skin, why she can talk to mummy without moving her lips, but she does know that daddy drank too much, that mummy isn't supposed to fall to the ground the way she did.

*Mummy! Mummy! Are you all right?*

She tries to read her mother's thoughts, but there are none.

"She was of no use to us, honey," says her father. "She would have just brought us down, don't you see that?"

"I thought you were gonna..."

Randolph shakes his head gently. "No, she could never be one of us. You are as I am because of my blood, the way I am because of my father's blood, and his mother's blood and so on."

"You..." tears would have welled in her eyes had she fed recently. "You killed Mummy..."

The little girl scans the room, her mind a torrent of fury and betrayal. All she wanted to do was make mummy feel better, to bring daddy back so they could all live together again, and what does he do? He kills her!

Greta bares her teeth in anger rather than the lust for blood that most often causes a vampire to bare their teeth.

From the dining room table she grabs the kerosene lamp and throws it at her father. He tries to avoid it, but in her fear she has developed another one of her powers: strength. And with that strength she lunges the lamp at blinding speed. It hits her father dead centre, splashing him with kerosene that engulfs with the flame instantaneously. She then tears the drapes from the picture window and throws them onto her father as he screams and flails about trying to extinguish the fire.

As he moves about the room he lights smaller fires on the furniture and the carpet, and when he tips over the other kerosene lamp it is a forgone conclusion.

Greta runs out the door in the wake of her father's screams. She stands there where he had been resurrected and watches as the house burns to the ground, his screams lasting far longer than they should have.

She has a long and strange life ahead of her, and she isn't sure what to do next, but she does know one thing: she is awfully hungry.

# No Man's Land

## Stephen Patrick

"Wanna know what scares me?" The flame from Private Burns' cigarette danced in the dim light of the earth and wood cave that served as their home in the trenches. "Wanna know what I think about at night in this godforsaken place?" Burns exhaled a cloud of smoke that twirled over the poker table fashioned from a broken spool. He leaned forward, resting his shaky hand on his knee. "Easy. I don't want to die all alone out here."

Private Abner Wilkens, sat across from him, a thin white plume of smoke snaking out between jagged yellow teeth. "Bloody hell, boy, there's a thousand boys beside you every day, afraid of the same thing. You're never gonna die alone out here in the trenches. There's always some poor soul beside you givin' up his ghost. The only thing that matters is taking one of theirs before they get one of ours."

Private Joseph Taylor sat to Wilkens' right, calming his fears with a warm bottle of wine. Taylor took a swig and joined in. "I ain't gonna see the one that gets me. That's what I'm afraid of. I wanna meet my maker face on, eye to eye."

"You'll never see it coming," answered Wilkens, still

looking at his cards. "That's why we're here while the rich boys stay home. Ain't that right, Sergen' Price? Guys like you belong back home, not sloggin' through the mud and the blood like this."

In the corner of the dugout, Sergeant William Price was busy wiping down his rifle. "You want to know what scares me?" Price reached into his left breast pocket and pulled out a brown-tinged photograph of a brunette in a frilly school dress. "Letting her down."

The photo made a quick trip through the hands of the other soldiers. Wilkens lingered over the picture, devouring her image. "If I had a gal like her, I'd keep myself out of harm's way. Hide when I could or spend my days with the cooks serving bully beef and handing out hard tack. No sense playin' out those foolish stunts of yours and leave your wife for another bloke."

"I promised Lucy I'd make her proud and that's what I intend to do."

"All right, Wilkens," interrupted Burns. "You've been in the Army the longest. What are you afraid of?"

Wilkens crushed his cigarette and tossed the butt into the dirt. "Listen up, boys. You wanna know what scares me?"

His answer was lost in the shriek of an incoming mortar shell. Sergeant Price and the two privates dove for cover. Wilkens did not move. He grabbed a new cigarette and covered the cards with his other hand.

The explosion rattled the wooden beams of their dugout. Dust dropped from the ceiling, adding a layer of filth to each of them. Price and the others picked themselves up, checking each other for injuries.

Wilkens was still seated at the table, the cigarette in his mouth broken cleanly in half. He spat the remainder out onto the floor. "It's not easy to explain." His eyes narrowed. "There's this thing out there. It's always huntin'. It's always huntin' and always hungry. I never seen it with my eyes, but I've seen what it does."

"Sure you have," interrupted Burns. "I heard stories like that when I was a kid. I didn't believe them then and I ain't gonna believe them out here. There's enough spook tales around us to scare any man without making up a story."

Wilkens grabbed Taylor's wine and finished it in one swallow. He continued, oblivious to Burns' comments. "It walks out there in the mud, feastin' on torn and tattered bodies. The lucky ones die outright. The others, I'd rather not talk about."

"The Reaper," added Burns, ashes dripping from the cigarette between his quivering fingers.

"Not even close, son. The Reaper takes you away. I'd meet the Reaper just to get outta here. This thing is the worst kind a scavenger, eating the corpses rotting around us, peeling them open for his meal. But for some, his kiss locks them here, strippin' away flesh and blood 'til you're trapped in this hell, walkin' beside him in the land o' corpses, hungry for a scrap of skin and muscle."

"That's it?" Taylor leaned back, a smile cutting across his face. "You're afraid of some ghost crawling along the battlefield? I guess it's better to be afraid of something that don't exist than something real."

Wilkens leaned forward. "Boy your age should listen to the folks around him. Might keep you out of trouble."

Sergeant Price grabbed a brush from his kit and scraped some mud from his boots. "Everyone's got a right to be scared, but we still do our jobs, no matter what's out there."

A tiny rap came at the entryway to their dugout. A

young boy stood in the doorway. He was covered in soot and dirt. He wore the blue wool jacket of a French soldier, but the sleeves were rolled into thick cuffs that hung down over his fingers. A small collection of buttons and beads adorned his dirty lapel, hanging from rough, fraying stitches. Some were familiar; the flashes or insignia of British or French soldiers. Others bore the spread eagle insignia of the Kaiser's finest troops. His grey pants were worn through at the knees and the cuffs on his legs were rolled up above mismatched leather boots.

"Hello, sirs. My name is Francois. I mean no disrespect, but I have some items that might be of interest to you." He held up a thread-bare canvas sack in his blackened hands.

Wilkens was on the boy in an instant. "He's a goddamn trench rat, robbin' the dead." Wilkens drew his bayonet and held it to the boy's throat.

Price raced to the boy's aid. "Private! Stand down, he's just a boy."

The boy remained calm despite the gleaming blade against his skin. His bright chestnut eyes looked up at the raging Wilkens.

"I am sorry, sir. The men from C Company said these things might belong to your men."

The boy held out his tiny hand. It held a locket belonging to Private O'Grady who had been killed by a mortar.

"He's just a thief, stealing from the dead!" Wilkens snatched the locket from the boy's hand. "How much have you kept?"

"None, sir, I am ... my family was..." The boy stammered, searching for the right words. "I am too small to fight, so I do the only thing I can. I read once how, in ancient times, women would strip the dead and return their possessions to their families. I want to honour those who fall, so that their sacrifice can be known and they can be properly mourned. I mean no offense."

Wilkens grabbed the canvas bag from the boy's hands and dumped it on the ground. He ran his hand over the boy's pockets and emptied the contents onto the ground with the rest. In the makeshift pile were Sergeant Halloway's diary, Corporal Saunders' engraved wrist watch, even the bible that belonged to Private Wolf, who had been the only voice of God in this Hell.

"How much more have you stolen?" asked Wilkens.

Price stepped between them and pulled the boy free. He glared at Wilkens before handing the boy his canteen. "Take a drink, son. We appreciate what you are doing, but you shouldn't be here."

The boy took a small sip and wiped his mouth, leaving a clean streak across his face. "It's okay, Sir. I am small and weak, but I do my work at night when the soldiers try to sleep."

"What's your name, son?" asked Price.

"Francois, sir. Francois Dumond."

Price held out his hand to the boy. "My name is William."

The next day, a dawn barrage shook them into action. Price led them through a foggy, smouldering maze to the edge of the trench where they looked out into no man's land. A haze hung in front of them like a curtain, surrounding a pair of dark scarecrows on the wire in front of them; a pair of German soldiers that had been killed during the night and left as a warning to any Germans that dared cross over during the night.

"Wait 'til they hit the wire. Don't waste your bullets while they're running."

A wooden post splintered beside Price's face, sending a spray of wood chips into the air. A second round thumped into the ground in front of him, as he focused in on a dozen shadows walked toward them through the haze. Gunshots rang out, up and down the line, as soldiers fired wildly at the shadows. Price squinted and held his breath, steadying his rifle as he joined the fight. Bullets chewed up the ground around him and he sank to the ground. When the shooting subsided, he looked up to return fire, but the shadows were moving away, pushed back by the British bullets lashing out from the safety of the trenches.

The British Commanders ordered Price's men over the top for an attack of their own. They surged forward, stepping over corpses in no man's land until the German lines came to life. A pair of German machine guns on a small ridge opened fire, sending Price's men into a water-filled crater for cover. The whistle to retreat cut through the chaos and Price ordered his men back to their lines.

As the others ran past him back to safety, a trio of German soldiers closed in on them. He fired two shots before his rifle jammed. He lodged his bayonet into the chest of the first one, before grabbing his trenching shovel. The surprised Germans fired in a panic, sending up a spray of dirt from the missed shots. Price's shovel slammed into the face of one soldier, crushing his nose and mouth before spinning away and landing edge first across the bridge of the last soldier's nose. Price sprinted through a maze of jagged wire and broken bodies to catch up with his men. After nineteen hours of combat, Price's squad ate and slept in the same trench they had defended for the past month.

Despite the frustration of an endless stalemate, Price did his best to bolster the spirit of his men. As their ranks dwindled, many men welcomed the appearance of the boy each morning. It helped them remember the fallen, but also why they were fighting. Although the men hated Francois' reason for visiting, his appearances became a welcome routine. They tolerated him because he brought home personal effects of the soldiers lost out in no man's land. The boy would empty his pockets and then stay for a bowl of stew or a slab of stale bread. Whenever possible, Price would reward Francois' hard work with some of his own rations.

At the end of the day, when the men prepared for another night on the line, Price would slip away to write a letter home.

"She means a lot to you?" Francois asked through teeth browned by the last of Price's chocolate rations.

"Lucy means everything to me," answered Price, still scribbling his letter. "That's why it's so important that I write these letters."

"Then why risk your life every day?"

"If I turned away from a fight or let another man take a bullet for me, I'd never be able to face her again."

"I may be young, but I see a lot. I've seen men cry for their mothers and I've seen men betray their closest friends for another second of life. I think Lucy would understand."

Price tucked Lucy's photo into his breast pocket.

"You've seen too much, my friend. Too much for a boy or a man. I could never ask her to understand all of this."

The next attack was supposed to be easy. A twelve hour artillery barrage would destroy the German trenches before the infantry strolled across no man's land to take over the German trenches.

Price was the first one up the ladder. Dirt and smoke hung in the air and made it difficult to see, but the others scrambled up behind him and over the pock-marked countryside. A wall of men marched forward, maintaining their steady lines.

After fifty yards, four German machine gun nests came to life with staccato pulses of gunfire. The German positions had survived the barrage. The British soldiers fell like corn before a scythe. Price scrambled for cover, ducking into a shallow crater torn open by an artillery blast. Wilkens and Burns followed him. Taylor was twenty feet behind them, clutching at a crimson stain on his chest.

"Cover me!" screamed Price as he raced toward Taylor.

Price slid to a stop in the mud beside Taylor, who slumped over and breathed in violent, blood-soaked spasms. Price looked back to the British lines, scanning the horizon for a medic. He never saw the bayonet until it was too late. A German soldier drove his bayonet through the small of Price's back. Price tried to turn and defend himself, but the pain was too intense.

The crimson blade jutted out of his belly for a moment and then it was gone. Price fell to his knees, only to feel the blade cut through him again, driving through his upper back and stealing the breath from his lungs. Satisfied that Price was finished, the German withdrew his blade and ran toward the British trenches.

Price clawed at his shirt pocket, longing to see Lucy's face once more. He fumbled with his mud-coated buttons until his entire body went slack and he fell face first into the mud. He groped through his memory, trying to recreate her face, so he could die with her image in his eyes. After a year of carrying her photo in his pocket, he died without remembering her face.

The dull tug of death pulled him away from no man's land. The pain was gone, replaced by a faint sense of weightlessness. He struggled to feel his hands or feet, but could not find them.Suddenly, he felt heavy, like he was sinking. He fell down and down until he slammed hard against something. Shells exploded above him and explosions thundered on both sides. It was dark and he was alone. His belly was whole again and strength flowed through his limbs.

"Welcome back, my friend."

Price followed the voice to his left. Francois knelt beside him. A tiny trickle of blood ran over his chin.

"What happened?" asked Price.

"You died."

"Is this heaven?" The horrible screams and acrid smoke told him otherwise.

"I could not let you rot on the ground, not with your dear Lucy waiting for you back home. I have saved you, my friend."

"Saved me?"

"Two hundred years ago, on another battlefield, I was given the gift that I now give to you. It is a kindness you truly deserve."

"What kindness? Another life?" asked Price.

"Not another life, but another chance. A chance to return to your Lucy."

"What about the others? My men?"

"They do not concern you, now. Your worries are beyond the trenches and the war, beyond living and dying. I have freed you from that."

"You're the demon that Wilkens was talking about."

"I'm no demon. I simply do what I must to survive and try every day to make the world a better place. Death is beneath me now. As long as I find the flesh that sustains me, I am free to do what I can to help. I ... hunt ... among the bodies for the flesh that sustains me. It is the only way to stop the pain. But I do not disgrace the living. I never feast on those whose souls have not been taken. But you were different, so I shared my gift with you. Now you are free to explore all that the world has to offer. Like me, you are beyond death."

"Beyond death?" Price's eyes filled with rage.

"You deserve this gift. To return to her."

"You've cursed me. Don't you see that?" Price turned away and slammed his fist into the dirt. "You've turned me into a monster."

"I've given you a chance to see Lucy again. How can that be a terrible thing? My gift is not to you, but to your love for Lucy. Return to her, make her proud of the man you were."

"Not like this. Don't you understand? I can't return to her. I'll never see her again. Lucy died three years ago from tuberculosis. It is only her memory that drives me."

"But what about the letters?"

"That's how I talk to her. At least, until I can see her again in heaven. Now you've taken that away from me."

Price stood up in the mud of no man's land. He looked to the west and saw the trenches of the British front line. To the east was the German line. He turned his back on Francois and headed north, away from everything he once knew, and out of no man's land.

# NIGHT TERRORS

# PRODUCT 9

### LINDSEY GODDARD

The distance from my back door to the chain link fence that borders my yard might as well be the Serengeti Plain. It's too far. Too out in the open. Ripe with predators, thirsty for my blood.

Mary stares at me with unspoken hope in her eyes, as if I might save the world today. Her long brown hair is pulled into a sloppy bun. Loose hairs frame a worried face as she surveys the situation through a small window near the top of the door.

Rex is a good dog, but not worth dying for. I contemplate how to say this to Mary without sounding like a coward. She bites her lip, hard enough to turn the outer edges white, peering through that window with tears forming in her eyes.

"His leash is stuck. It's tangled in the wires of the fence. Ray ... he needs help..."

I motion with my fingers for her to step aside. Sunlight pours through the pane of glass, causing me to squint as I scan the area. I spot him in the distance. His black fur creates an easy target against the green and yellow foliage of the lawn. A shadow passes over him, blots out the sun for a fleeting moment. Clouds don't move like that, and I gulp, knowing damn well what Mary wants me to do.

Rex looks pathetic, tangled in the fence, whimpering as he senses the danger all around. This doesn't change the fact that the dumb-ass did this to himself. I shake my head. We have a routine around here, a daily regimen. A structured plan for every course of action. It keeps us safe. As safe as we can possibly be since the whole world went to hell. Rex knows the drill. He knows our routine like the back of his paw. But he messed up, went chasing that rabbit...

Once every morning and again every afternoon I crack the back door just wide enough for Rex to slip through. His leash is nothing more than a thin piece of rope, but it offers a certain level of stealth that his old jangly chain could not. I allow him a few feet of slack, just enough for him to do his business in the nearest patch of weeds. A large wooden deck provides shelter from predators: winged creatures that swoop down from the sky, plucking their prey from the ground. The hair on Rex's spine always stands straight up as he watches the tall weeds for signs of movement. He knows I'm eager for him to finish, to bring him back inside. But I guess no matter how much a dog adapts to human life, in the end, a dog is simply a dog. All it took was a moment of canine instinct, a gut response to visual stimuli that clouded Rex's judgment for one second. *See rabbit. Want rabbit. Chase rabbit.* Just like that. He yanked the leash hard enough to rip it from my grasp, and took off across the untrimmed grass.

Mary looks at me, tortured thoughts causing the wrinkles around her eyes to deepen. She pulls on her fingers, nervously. After twenty years of marriage I still find her beautiful. The soft nape of her neck as she tilts her head to the side, waiting for my response. The long, black lashes that frame her tired eyes. Like any stupid male with too much testosterone churning through his veins, I will risk it all, just to see her smile.

"I'll get him," I mutter, because there's nothing else to say. No other answer will suffice. Rex is her baby, and I've got to bring him home.

It's the response she's been goading me for, and yet the words seem to upset her. She bites her lip again, hanging her head. With a long sigh, she stares at the floor, thinking. "There's a million thoughts going through my head. I keep debating if it's worth the risk…"

"And?"

"I don't know, Ray. I really don't. I couldn't live another minute if something happened to you. I'd probably join you in death, if I could manage. But look at him…" Her voice trails off as she gazes through the window.

I inch up behind her, resting my palms on her shoulders. I lay my head against her soft brown hair, sprinkled with strands of grey. I sigh and softly say, "It's fine. We have travelled further than this, not so many days ago. I can make it."

I feel her muscles tighten beneath my fingers, hard to the touch. "Take the shotgun," she whispers, breathily. I kiss her neck before I turn and walk away.

Mary and I were never able to have children. Try as we might, it just wasn't in the cards. All around, the Earth was crumbling due to overpopulation. That the burgeoning human race is what caused this hell … it felt like a slap in the face. We weren't allowed the joy of procreation. Yet, we had to suffer the consequences of a world overrun by humans.

Over the years, Mary focused her pent-up maternal

energy on whatever lucky furball served as the family pet. Currently that was Rex, and she loved him dearly. Her heart would break if I let him die today.

Rounding the corner from the main room to the hallway, I pause and look back at Mary. Her vision is still fixed on the tiny window. I know she misses the view from her upstairs kitchen, with its large bay window and sliding glass doors that lead out to the red cedar deck. There are only a few oddly placed windows in the basement, casting eerie beams of light through the dusty atmosphere. It works for me. I've seen those things shatter glass, ramming into it repeatedly until a thousand shards scatter the ground. But they aren't small enough to fit through the basement windows. So this is where we spend our days. Downstairs.

Halfway down the hall and to the left is the laundry room, which also serves as a storage area for essential items. Flipping open a cabinet, I grab the shotgun holster and fasten it to my back. I slide the shotgun into place. I study the myriad of hunting and pocket knives, selecting one with a leather sheath. I strap it to my thigh and grab my combat boots. The laces go knee-high, fitting the leather snugly to my calves.

Mary flashes me a worried look as I saunter back in. I try not to look uneasy as I stroll over to the door, peer through the little window. Rex is still hooked to the fence. His flat, pink tongue hangs from his mouth as he pants, sunlight illuminating the green leaves that weave through the metal wires behind him. Mary walks over, plants a kiss on my cheek, and whispers in my ear, "Please hurry."

I slip outside, making sure I hear the door latch behind me. It's cool and breezy in the shade of the deck. I listen for any signs of approaching danger, twigs crushing in the distance, wings fluttering overhead. All I hear is a soft breeze rattling through the branches of surrounding trees, and Rex whimpering at the edge of the yard. I inch stealthily past the edge of shadow, into the sunlight. Into the open. My throat seems to go dry and shrivel inside my neck, but I swallow hard, thinking back on how this whole mess began.

It started with the WPS. That stands for "World Population Society". They set up headquarters in every one of the fifty states. Their goal? A solution to the noticeable strain our growing human race put on the environment. Each WPS building was surrounded by dense military quarters and shrouded in secrecy. Until they released Product 9.

They had been working on an answer to the diminishing food supply. They claimed this powder form of sustenance was the key. It tasted bland, nothing to rave about, but tolerable to the average pallet. They had tested Product 9 on various forms of animals, namely mammals. The results were always the same: a sustained and nourished body for much longer than the average meal. And the ingredients required very few natural crops. Our problems were solved.

But there was an outcome, unforeseen to the scientists who developed Product 9. The experiments went well while contained inside the WPS headquarters. The test runs produced satisfactory results, but soon the product was released. Available on every store shelf, every city. Remnants of it tossed into every dumpster. Soon the bugs began to eat it. That's when people took notice. The bugs ... they were starting to grow.

Beetles the size of field mice, sometimes larger than rats, were spotted at parks and camp sites. Cockroaches as long as the human foot infested the dumps of the city. Stomping on the mutant bugs was less preferable than simply walking away. Killing them left a revolting mess of splintered exoskeleton, pale white innards, and translucent slime. In dark alleyways, you could hear them scuttle. The pitter patter of little feet that sounded too hard, like the tapping of fingernails on a desk.

People started staying indoors. On shopping trips, they would fill two or three carts with whatever cans hadn't been discontinued during the reign of Product 9, in hopes of waiting out the problem. Some people turned to looting and violence. Some people found God. Others got drunk or high.

The WPS and other government agencies promised a quick, clean solution, but never seemed to deliver. Things worsened day by day, until the average housefly had to be swatted away with an aluminium baseball bat and children were getting mauled by cockroaches. Mary and I had a chunk of money we'd been saving for retirement. We cleaned out our savings account, stocking up on everything we could possibly need. We haven't left the house since that day.

Until now.

I am running at full speed, fresh beads of sweat forming on my skin. It feels good to have the sun on my face again. It's been weeks. Yet, I'm not covering the open area as quickly as I'd hoped. The spacious back yard had been a selling point when Mary and I purchased the house years ago. Now it seems like the worst mistake I've ever made.

Rex stands, wagging his tail. He yanks at the rope, probably only managing to tighten the knots further. That's okay. I have my trusty knife.

A shadow passes overhead, and I immediately crouch,

shielding myself with one arm and reaching for my knife with the other. I hear a buzzing. It's the sound of giant wings flapping at one thousand beats per second. I look up, and I can see its fat body. Its iridescent shell changes from green to blue to black as it swoops through the air. Long, thick hairs jut out in every direction from its back, making strange patterns across the clouds. Like a boomerang, it changes direction as it passes and begins to head back my way. I contemplate whether to reach for my gun. The blast will alert other insects to my presence. I'll only use it as a last resort.

Huge, red eyes bulge from its head with intense detail. I see the tiny sections of its compound eyes, like a close-up photo I once saw in a book. I cannot tell where its vision is fixed. It could be looking down at me, watching its potential meal, or possibly looking straight ahead in search of something else. There's no way to be sure. So I stay perfectly still, breath shallow in my lungs, until its translucent wings carry it far enough away that I'm sure it's no longer a threat.

My knees are trembling as I stand. *God damn house flies are as big as a house!* I shake my head. Rex is going to owe me, big time. If I could send him outside to fetch the paper, he'd be doing it every day for the rest of his life. Too bad the paper boy never comes anymore. Too bad Rex can't go outside to fetch a thing.

I throw myself into a high-speed run. I haven't ran like this since my football days. My heart is pounding in my chest with such force, I feel like it might burst through my ribs. A cramp forms in my side, burning its way up the opposing rib cage. My arms are pumping furiously. Trickles of sweat run down my flesh, pooling in the crevices and folds of my body, soaking my clothes.

I draw near to Rex. His tail is nothing but a frantic blur as it whips from side to side. I examine the rope that's twisted through the grid-like fence, and I notice something. I hadn't seen it from the distance. Heavy braids of crystalline thread are woven into the shrubs, strewn about the metal fence. In areas where this thread-like material is thickest, it appears white, gauzy, like the bushes have been bandaged. Approaching the fence, I reach out and touch the tip of my finger to one of the gigantic threads. It sticks to my finger, pulling my skin as I recoil in disgust. A spider web.

"What have you gotten me into, boy?" I scold.

One hand gripping the rope, I use my other hand to unsheathe the knife, fumbling with both as my nerves take over. Raw spots of skin dot Rex's fur coat, little patches of pink where there's usually black. The hair has been ripped away during his struggle with the sticky web.

Silken strands entwine the fence where the rope is tangled. I position the knife and make a clean slice, leaving only two feet of leash dangling from Rex's collar. We both look at each other for a fraction of a second before sprinting towards the house at full speed.

I sense movement behind us. I write it off as paranoia, the way a person can feel their skin crawl after seeing a swarm of insects. Then, something blots out the sun. A huge shadow spreads over the yard, and I'm in the centre of it, running.

I turn my head to glance over my shoulder. Climbing over the shrubs from the yard adjacent to mine is a spindly arachnid with a plump, furry mid-section. Its head is raised high, sunlight framing its face like a demented halo, eight beady eyes locked on me. It's still working its huge body over the fence, moving with grace across the dense, sticky patches of thread. Each slender leg has two joints, two knees, where it bends, allowing it to skitter over obstacles with ease. Two fangs protrude from its maw, taking up half its face. I think I see one of them drip.

Still running, I pull the shotgun from its holster. It hurts when I twist around to aim. Something pops and then burns in my spine. I pay no attention to it, sending a shotgun blast across the yard towards the spider as it closes in on me. The shot misses, blows a hole in the bushes. Little pieces of splintered wood and fragments of leaves swirl behind the enclosing monster.

I cock the shotgun again, slow my pace so I can steady the barrel. This blast throws my shoulder back, as I'm running out of strength. I see chunks of flesh explode from the spider's abdomen, landing in sickening hunks in the grass and leaving a dent in its bulbous midriff.

Silently, without so much as a cry, its skinny legs stop moving, body rigid. I hold my breath, looking forward, still running. Getting closer.

I close the gap between myself and the door, looking behind me in time to see the spider slinking away. It drags its wounded body over the gauzy bushes, mounting the fence, dropping soundlessly out of sight.

The door swings open and Mary steps aside, allowing a wide berth for us to spill through the entry. I fall to my knees and praise the safe refuge. She slams the door, locks it, runs to me. Encircles me with her arms.

I hear Rex whimpering, Mary sobbing with joy. My heart is thumping so loudly in my ears it's a miracle I can hear anything at all. I hug her close, and she kisses me all over my face. I look into her hazel eyes, which appear green in the dim light of the basement, fresh tears shimmering on their surface.

"You are the bravest man I've ever known, and the sweetest," she says, holding my face in her hands.

Rex pushes his big, furry head underneath our trembling arms and joins the reunion. His flat, gritty tongue is lapping at Mary's face and trying to reach mine. I keep his saliva-coated mouth at bay with my forearm, as Mary continues to work her fingers through my hair, gently stroking. I feel her hot breath on my sweat-dampened skin and savour her familiar aroma.

Rex is a good dog, but not worth dying for. Yet, this woman ... she is. And I would.

## 🕷 Classic Break 🕷

# The Tell-Tale Heart

### Edgar Allan Poe

TRUE! nervous, very, very dreadfully nervous I had been and am; but why *will* you say that I am mad? The disease had sharpened my senses, not destroyed, not dulled them. Above all was the sense of hearing acute. I heard all things in the heaven and in the earth. I heard many things in hell. How then am I mad? Hearken! And observe how healthily, how calmly, I can tell you the whole story.

It is impossible to say how first the idea entered my brain, but, once conceived, it haunted me day and night. Object there was none. Passion there was none. I loved the old man. He had never wronged me. He had never given me insult. For his gold I had no desire. I think it was his eye! Yes, it was this! One of his eyes resembled that of a vulture — a pale blue eye with a film over it. Whenever it fell upon me my blood ran cold, and so by degrees, very gradually, I made up my mind to take the life of the old man, and thus rid myself of the eye for ever.

Now this is the point. You fancy me mad. Madmen know nothing. But you should have seen me. You should have seen how wisely I proceeded — with what caution — with what foresight, with what dissimulation, I went to work! I was never kinder to the old man than during the whole week before I killed him. And every night about midnight I turned the latch of his door and opened it oh, so gently! And then, when I had made an opening sufficient for my head, I put in a dark lantern all closed, closed so that no light shone out, and then I thrust in my head. Oh, you would have laughed to see how cunningly I thrust it in! I moved it slowly, very, very slowly, so that I might not disturb the old man's sleep. It took me an hour to place my whole head within the opening so far that I could see him as he lay upon his bed. Ha! Would a madman have been so wise as this? And then when my head was well in the room I undid the lantern cautiously — oh, so cautiously — cautiously (for the hinges creaked), I undid it just so much that a single thin ray fell upon the vulture eye. And this I did for seven long nights, every night just at midnight, but I found the eye always closed, and so it was impossible to do the work, for it was not the old man who vexed me but his Evil Eye. And every morning, when the day broke, I went boldly into the chamber and spoke courageously to him, calling him by name in a hearty tone, and inquiring how he had passed the night. So you see he would have been a very profound old man, indeed, to suspect that every night, just at twelve, I looked in upon him while he slept.

Upon the eighth night I was more than usually cautious in opening the door. A watch's minute hand moves more quickly than did mine. Never before that night had I felt the extent of my own powers, of my sagacity. I could scarcely contain my feelings of triumph. To think that there I was opening the door little by little, and he not even to dream of my secret deeds or thoughts. I fairly chuckled at the idea, and perhaps he heard me, for he moved on the bed suddenly as if startled. Now you may think that I drew back — but no. His room was as black as pitch with the thick darkness (for the shutters were close fastened through fear of robbers), and so I knew that he could not see the opening of the door, and I kept pushing it on steadily, steadily.

I had my head in, and was about to open the lantern, when my thumb slipped upon the tin fastening, and the old man sprang up in the bed, crying out, "Who's there?"

I kept quite still and said nothing. For a whole hour I did not move a muscle, and in the meantime I did not hear him lie down. He was still sitting up in the bed, listening; just as I have done night after night hearkening to the death watches in the wall.

Presently, I heard a slight groan, and I knew it was the groan of mortal terror. It was not a groan of pain or of grief — oh, no! It was the low stifled sound that arises from the bottom of the soul when overcharged with awe. I knew the sound well. Many a night, just at midnight, when all the world slept, it has welled up from my own bosom, deepening, with its dreadful echo, the terrors that distracted me. I say I knew it well. I knew what the old man felt, and pitied him although I chuckled at heart. I knew that he had been lying awake ever since the first slight noise when he had turned in the bed. His fears had been ever since growing upon him. He had been trying to fancy them causeless, but could not. He had been saying to himself, "It is nothing but the wind in the chimney, it is only a mouse crossing the floor," or, "It is merely a cricket which has made a single chirp." Yes, he has been trying to comfort himself with these suppositions; but he had found all in vain. *All in vain*, because Death in approaching him had stalked with his black shadow before him and enveloped the victim. And it was the mournful influence of the unperceived shadow that caused him to feel, although he neither saw nor heard, to feel the presence of my head within the room.

When I had waited a long time very patiently without hearing him lie down, I resolved to open a little — a very, very little crevice in the lantern. So I opened it — you cannot imagine how stealthily, stealthily — until at length a single dim ray like the thread of the spider shot out from the crevice and fell upon the vulture eye.

It was open, wide, wide open, and I grew furious as I gazed upon it. I saw it with perfect distinctness — all a dull blue with a hideous veil over it that chilled the very marrow in my bones, but I could see nothing else of the old man's face or person, for I had directed the ray as if by instinct precisely upon the damned spot.

And now have I not told you that what you mistake for madness is but over-acuteness of the senses? Now, I say, there came to my ears a low, dull, quick sound, such as a watch makes when enveloped in cotton. I knew that sound well too. It was the beating of the old man's heart. It increased my fury as the beating of a drum stimulates the soldier into courage.

But even yet I refrained and kept still. I scarcely breathed. I held the lantern motionless. I tried how steadily I could maintain the ray upon the eye. Meantime the hellish tattoo of the heart increased. It grew quicker and quicker, and louder and louder, every instant. The old man's terror must have been extreme! It grew louder, I say, louder every moment! Do you mark me well? I have told you that I am nervous: so I am. And now at the dead hour of the night, amid the dreadful silence of that old house, so strange a noise as this excited me to uncontrollable terror.

Yet, for some minutes longer I refrained and stood still. But the beating grew louder, louder! I thought the heart must burst. And now a new anxiety seized me — the sound would be heard by a neighbour! The old man's hour had come! With a loud yell, I threw open the lantern and leaped into the room. He shrieked once — once only. In an instant I dragged him to the floor, and pulled the heavy bed over him. I then smiled gaily, to find the deed so far done. But for many minutes the heart beat on with a muffled sound. This, however, did not vex me; it would not be heard through the wall. At length it ceased. The old man was dead. I removed the bed and examined the corpse. Yes, he was stone, stone dead. I placed my hand upon the heart and held it there many minutes. There was no pulsation. He was stone dead. His eye would trouble me no more.

If still you think me mad, you will think so no longer when I describe the wise precautions I took for the concealment of the body. The night waned, and I worked hastily, but in silence.

I took up three planks from the flooring of the chamber, and deposited all between the scantlings. I then replaced the boards so cleverly so cunningly, that no human eye — not even his — could have detected anything wrong. There was nothing to wash out — no stain of any kind — no blood-spot whatever. I had been too wary for that.

When I had made an end of these labours, it was four o'clock — still dark as midnight. As the bell sounded the hour, there came a knocking at the street door. I went down to open it with a light heart, — for what had I now to fear? There entered three men, who introduced themselves, with perfect suavity, as officers of the police. A shriek had been heard by a neighbour during the night;

suspicion of foul play had been aroused; information had been lodged at the police office, and they (the officers) had been deputed to search the premises.

I smiled — for what had I to fear? I bade the gentlemen welcome. The shriek, I said, was my own in a dream. The old man, I mentioned, was absent in the country. I took my visitors all over the house. I bade them search — search well. I led them, at length, to his chamber. I showed them his treasures, secure, undisturbed. In the enthusiasm of my confidence, I brought chairs into the room, and desired them here to rest from their fatigues, while I myself, in the wild audacity of my perfect triumph, placed my own seat upon the very spot beneath which reposed the corpse of the victim.

The officers were satisfied. My *manner* had convinced them. I was singularly at ease. They sat and while I answered cheerily, they chatted of familiar things. But, ere long, I felt myself getting pale and wished them gone. My head ached, and I fancied a ringing in my ears; but still they sat, and still chatted. The ringing became more distinct: I talked more freely to get rid of the feeling: but it continued and gained definitiveness — until, at length, I found that the noise was *not* within my ears.

No doubt I now grew *very* pale; but I talked more fluently, and with a heightened voice. Yet the sound increased — and what could I do? It was *a low, dull, quick sound — much such a sound as a watch makes when enveloped in cotton.* I gasped for breath, and yet the officers heard it not. I talked more quickly, more vehemently but the noise steadily increased. I arose and argued about trifles, in a high key and with violent gesticulations; but the noise steadily increased. Why *would* they not be gone? I paced the floor to and fro with heavy strides, as if excited to fury by the observations of the men, but the noise steadily increased. Oh God! What *could* I do? I foamed — I raved — I swore! I swung the chair upon which I had been sitting, and grated it upon the boards, but the noise arose over all and continually increased. It grew louder — louder — louder! And still the men chatted pleasantly, and smiled. Was it possible they heard not? Almighty God! — No, no? They heard! — They suspected! — They *knew*! — They were making a mockery of my horror! — This I thought, and this I think. But anything was better than this agony! Anything was more tolerable than this derision! I could bear those hypocritical smiles no longer! I felt that I must scream or die! And now — again — hark! Louder! Louder! Louder! *Louder*!

"Villains!" I shrieked. "Dissemble no more! I admit the deed! Tear up the planks — here, here — it is the beating of his hideous heart!"

# NIGHT TERRORS

# SHARE THE LOVE

## CHRIS DONAHUE

Dr. Weiss snapped awake, feeling the ground shake under him. "No," he groaned as a second and third shock followed the first.

He rolled off his cot with an agility at odds with his fifty-four years of a mostly quiet life. He climbed onto his lab bench and grabbed the bars protecting his ground-floor window. The rising sun put a rosy glow on the impact craters less than three miles away.

A fourth meteor blazed down to strike the west end of the valley. It was overkill. The hidden hospital as well as the bunker-like buildings of the farm were now craters surrounded by flames before the fourth strike.

"Emma," he whispered as he felt like a knife twisted in his chest. But nothing as merciful as a knife waited for him. His wife and newborn daughter were now ash and a protein smoke; as were a dozen other mothers and the starving outpost's last chance at feeding itself.

Weiss squatted on the bench, back to the wall, and held his head. His beautiful wife and partner was gone and all they had struggled to survive seemed pointless. For once, he wished he shared her faith and its Other-worldly focus.

She had inexplicably combined a sharp scientific mind with an unshakable faith in God. Over the years, he had come to trust her instincts. Even if he didn't understand her moral compass, he'd used her as his own.

No longer. Now she was gone, along with most of the Survivor's medical team.

The lab door burst open. Falconni, assault rifle angling from his hip, locked eyes with Weiss. "Doc, I'm sorry, man. No idea how they found the hospital, but we need you and what's left of the Council. Now, down by the gym."

Weiss nodded. He wanted to scream at the Scout Team Leader, but that would be unreasonable. He wanted to curl into a ball and die, but that comfort wasn't in him either. Emma would have known what to do. She would've found a way to go on if he had just died. Not even at the height of the Zombie Plague had he felt so adrift.

He wanted the universe to feel his pain. The tickle of an idea told him he should do just that and damn the consequences. Emma had absolutely forbidden him to continue his viral experiments when he told her of his promising tests on a new weapon. Trusting her, he had shelved the idea. But, now she was gone and he lacked her abiding faith that something else, something better, would save them in time.

"I'm on my way," he said as if Falconni had just caught him writing up notes after an experiment. Calm, radiate calm, he thought. It's expected of you.

As Weiss followed Falconni down the hall, he tried not to think about the sheer injustice of it all. He and Emma had beat horrific odds and survived the Zombie Plague. They had been the core of this group who held a fortified research centre near the Camp David government retreats. They and their people outlasted the teeming hordes of fresh zombies and the dangerous years after when only dwindling numbers of nearly-human zombies still roamed.

They survived roaming bands of marauders, more vicious than the hungry undead. They had even survived the bombardments by the aliens who had created and unleashed the Zombie Plague. Nine months ago, Emma believed the worst was over and they had an obligation to rebuild humanity. And he foolishly agreed. She had been right, without empiric evidence, before.

Until today, they had both survived everything the Universe had thrown at them. He felt a red rage flare. But, Dr. Michael Weiss wasn't a man given to berserker hysterics.

Falconni waved a few people aside as he led Weiss to the gym. Survivors knew when to shut up and get out of the way. Weiss appreciated the way the last six years of disasters had gotten people to focus on what mattered and not on how they felt or how they could inflict their own prejudices on the rest of humanity. Sadly it had taken near-extinction to accomplish this miracle.

He fought back a shiver. It was too soon to call what they faced merely 'near'.

The Council's eight-seat table in the gym was surrounded by a dozen Survivors trying to remain calm. Colbert, a Navy Engineer before the Plague and Ms. Karsten the Chief Administrator were already seated. Both looked as shaken as Weiss had ever seen them.

"I'm sorry about Emma, Mike," Colbert said softly as Weiss sat down. "She wasn't alone. I thought the place was invisible from above. Damn."

Colbert continued, speaking to the gathering crowd, "Look, I don't know how they found the hospital and farm. The heat shielding and camouflage there were the same as we have here. All I do know is that if they'd spotted us here, we'd be a crater, too."

"Losing the hospital was bad," Karsten's grating voice wasn't smoothed by the desperation underneath, "but even with the farm we were barely going to make it. Without the farm, we have no more than a month's worth of food left."

Weiss ignored the anxious faces around him and pointed at Falconni, "Do we know if there are any survivors?"

"My team and Jackson's guys are headed there now. But, you saw the hit. Nothing's left. Nobody made it out of that."

Someone pushed through the crowd to stand in front of Weiss and the others. Of course, Davis. If anyone was going to complain about a new rationing level or a new work draft, it would be Davis. He always managed to be somewhere else when patrols were assigned, yet the former congressional aide could be counted on being first in line if a cache of food turned up. "So, are we fucked now?"

Weiss glanced at the other Councillors, "Yes, we are."

A blank look replaced Davis's usual surly grimace. Any other time, Weiss would have chuckled at finally hitting on a way to shut Davis up. In previous disasters, the Councillors trying to keep the people calm merely acted as a challenge to Davis and his trio of supporters.

"What do you mean, 'Yes, we're fucked'?" He stomped and looked around at the growing crowd of frightened faces. "You're in charge. You're supposed to fix it. What do we do now?"

Karsten shrugged, "We have three, maybe four weeks of food left at starvation rations. The farm is gone. We've long-since scavenged any canned or dried food stores in this part of the state. Even if it wouldn't be bombed, we haven't the seed or stock to start a new farm."

"They didn't hit the Shop," said Colbert. "We can still turn out bullets, grenades, simple rockets and gas bombs and keep the trucks running for a while. But, none of that is very good eating."

Weiss ignored Davis, but glanced across the rest of the people. "Unless the aliens threw in some unknown virus, your inoculations should prevent any new zombie outbreaks."

He drew in a breath before adding, "It won't bring back the farm or bring back those we lost with the hospital, but I've been working on something new to make the aliens suffer. Hear me out, there is a risk. But, as I see it, we have to change our current paradigm or face extinction."

That brought calm, of a feral sort, to the group.

This was where Emma would have stood up and voiced some moral objection. He felt the silence like a wound.

"Falconni," Weiss called, "Gather the teams. If I have the Council's approval to proceed, I'll need you to bring in at least three of the alien males, three females and six neuters."

Colbert and Karsten nodded. The angry growl from the rest of the people favoured anything taking suffering to the aliens who had brought the Zombie Plague and the past year of bombardment and starvation.

The Team Leader nodded, "Okay. Three Bulls, three Cows and six Sticks. We'll have to hit a couple of convoys or one of their outposts." With a curl on his lip, he added, "If we're real lucky, we'll snag some alien chow at the same time. Martinez, Schwartz, gather your men and come with me."

"They're coming down Culpepper Lane," Alex called softly to Falconni while sliding down the rubble pile that had once been the wall of a drugstore. Chen remained above, keeping an eye out for zombies, aliens or any other form of trouble. Alex hit the bottom and checked the hook at the end of his left arm, then continued his report, "Looks like five aliens total; three Sticks, a Bull and a Cow. They're in a chopped-up SUV with two gun mounts. Probably bringing groceries to an outpost."

"Good," answered Falconni. "That's the kind of mix of aliens Dr. Weiss said he wanted. We can even lose one of the Sticks and still be okay."

Under the clear noon sun, the three men of Falconni's team gave slight shrugs or casual grins. They'd miss taking out the alien-driven vehicle with a Molotov Cocktail. That kind of attack offered little risk, plus the entertainment value of watching aliens dance and scream as their flesh melted away. But, like Falconni, his men were convinced the tests Dr. Weiss wanted to perform would make any captured aliens wish they'd simply been burned alive.

Tapping Hugo on the shoulder, Falconni said, "Three here, two of us on the other side." Then he headed for the storm sewer running under Culpepper.

As any Survivor would, Falconni took a deep sniff before entering the concrete tunnel. It had been nearly a year since he'd last seen, or smelled, a fresh zombie but old habits died hard. No human still alive would step into the dark without tensing. Most of the zombies had rotted away years ago, but enough remained to be a threat on top of everything else.

A quick scramble through the sewer over damp, decaying vegetation and booting a couple of rats out of the way got them into position before the alien vehicle reached the trap.

Falconni tucked his head low as he heard the SUV's tyres crunching down Culpepper. The aliens had modified an old SUV for their use. Like so much else, the aliens didn't bring many of their own vehicles, using human equipment and taking over the empty remains of human cities and factories.

The strip of nail-studded rubber laid across the road was under a covering of dust and patches of dried grass. Two pairs of tyres blew out in quick succession and the men launched themselves out of their weed-choked ditch.

One of the Sticks, a tall, slender blue alien, fought to control the rusted Explorer as it twisted to its left, toward Falconni.

The two other luckless Sticks tried to stay balanced in their gunner positions standing up through the roof. One of the vaguely humanoid aliens gripped a ring-mounted M-16 much the way a human soldier in a Hummer might work a .50 calibre machine gun. Human bullets sprayed wildly from the gun. The other alien gunner lost its balance and banged its head on the fragile glass and copper alien beam weapon mounted on the back ring.

The Stick in the rear position fired a wild shot. A beam of bright green light punched a one inch hole cleanly through the telephone pole Falconni ducked behind. "Damn," Falconni cursed reflexively as he touched the cold place where his right earlobe had existed an instant before. Nothing turned those deadly beams, fortunately the weapons required several seconds to recharge.

The SUV nearly tipped over as the driver ploughed into

a bolted down mailbox. Falconni reached into the stopped SUV and dragged the stunned driver out through the glass-less driver's window. Dr. Weiss specified live captives, but banged up a bit would do just fine.

Falconni heard the electric snap of the alien beam weapon again. Hugo pulled the struggling rear gunner out of its ring while Anderson jumped up from the far side to push the front gunner's weapon down and out of the alien's grip.

The blue-skinned creature gave a catlike yowl as Anderson punched it in the chest with his good hand before pulling it out of the SUV with his hook through the alien's harness. Givens yanked open a back door and prodded a shorter alien out. The four-foot tall creature seemed squat compared to her seven-foot neuter companions. Like her, they weighed around one hundred and twenty pounds and wore dazed expressions enhanced by the jerky motion of the slender antennae waving between their brows. The unarmed alien female stayed silent.

Behind Givens, Chen lay with a one-inch hole through his throat. The flash-cauterised wound didn't bleed, but the recent addition to the Survivors group was dead.

It took no effort to bring the last passenger out. The Bull stood his full four and one-half foot height, his four-fingered hands and thick, horn-like antennae quivering with rage. "You animals have no right," the translator pin said in slow, steady English. Based on the torrent of squeaks and growls coming from the Bull, the pin probably edited curses and threats. No matter.

Dr. Weiss particularly needed a healthy Bull. So, Falconni would deliver one feisty alien male.

"You will release us, immediately," the translator pin

said without inflection.

Givens slung his weapon and hoisted the one hundred and forty pound Bull easily, ignoring its squeal of protest. "I'd let you go if y'all would go all the ways home an' leave us alone fo' good."

"This world is ours, now. Your time is over. Just die," the pin said slowly. The Bull's jerking antennae and flaring nose flaps telling a more passionate version than the translation.

"Seems y'all gets to do some dyin' first," Givens said.

Arguing with aliens was pointless. They acted as if human attacks were the height of rudeness and seemed unable to comprehend the human desire for revenge. The few aliens Falconni bothered to interrogate took the fact that any humans survived the Plague as an unforgivable insult. Their weakness as soldiers went a long way to explain why they'd used biological warfare and space bombardment to try and exterminate humanity before setting up colonies. That didn't leave a lot of room for negotiation.

"Falconni," Hugo barked, tilting his head up Culpepper.

A zombie crawled through the broken window of a dress store some thirty feet away. The zombie's shrunken eyes and shrivelled muscles gave the false impression it was nearly blind and completely weak. A fool might think that, if it were six years ago before the Plague.

Falconni recognised her as one of the few truly dangerous kinds of zombies left. Ones that had fed so well during that first week of the Plague that she was nearly human again. Most zombie victims had rotted away before they could gorge on living human flesh and extend their unnatural lives. This one had been luckier than most; if years of starving in a nearly-human state while the food source you craved dwindled and became more dangerous, could be called lucky.

"Not this time," Falconni said as Hugo raised his AK-47 for a shot at the zombie. "You know, Hugo," Falconni added in a conversational tone, "Dr. Weiss only needs two Sticks for our group and yours looks pretty dinged-up."

With a grin, Hugo hoisted the Stick who'd killed Chen, by the harness that made up the alien's only clothing. "You're right, Falconni. I'd be totally embarrassed to take this specimen to the Doc, what with its forehead all bloody and all."

Falconni's fifteen-year-old soldier slammed the Stick against the Explorer's rusted side, breaking one of the alien's hollow-boned thighs against the solid frame. Hugo then shoved the squealing Stick ten feet towards the cautiously approaching zombie.

Falconni jabbed the two remaining Sticks with his rifle until they hoisted Chen's body between them. The zombie's bite would not bring him back now, but Falconni wouldn't leave one of his own behind.

"Givens, grab that supply chest from the SUV. There might be something in it we can use." Alien foods were almost inedible. But, when the alternative was no food at all, 'almost' is an important word.

Holding his now very docile Stick by a harness strap, Falconni led his team and captives back to their base and Dr. Weiss.

The injured Stick screeched, trying to crawl after them as the desiccated zombie eased closer. The zombie would feed on the Stick, getting little more of the nourishment it craved from the alien's flesh than it did from the rats the zombie ate to keep itself barely alive. Like the rats, the Stick would remain dead after the zombie finished with it.

The virus in the zombie's bite, as tailored by the aliens, only affected humans.

Dr. Weiss glanced at Falconni's catch. "Well done, young man. I see you lost a soldier, sorry. Put the male and female in cage fourteen. Secure them with these," he said, handing Falconni a handful of nylon ties. "You can deposit the neuters in the central pen. The other teams brought in more than enough. Falconni winked at Weiss's assistant, Claire, "You've got it, Doc." She was only three years older than Falconni and reasonably attractive. Weiss felt a sharp pang as he remembered being much more awkward when he first spoke to Emma, so many years ago.

Silently, Weiss wished Falconni luck with Claire. The Team Leader seemed very competent, particularly for a former rock band roadie. Women had made up less than one sixth of the Survivors from the original Zombie Plague. When the aliens arrived to claim a human-cleansed Earth, they dropped meteors from space onto the fort-like settlements most humans had clustered in, killing many more women and infinitely precious children. Those few women remaining were encouraged to have as many children as possible.

Weiss fought back the urge to bellow like a wounded animal. His wife and child were dead! But, he grabbed onto the rage. He would need that strength soon.

The dry, underground pool used as a captive Holding area had cyclone fence pens around the sides of its crumbling basin, adequate for most of the physically weak aliens. Falconni's team secured the agitated alien male to a post bolted to the floor and strapped the female to a wooden bench where three neuters were already in place.

Weiss had spent most of his life as an unemotional scientist. He and his people needed his calm reason and medical skills during the Zombie Plague and the trying times afterward. But now, as he looked down at the aliens in their cages, he felt a burning hatred. Almost immediately, the calm, analytical part of his brain promised him his revenge. He would know soon. He smiled.

In the corner of each of the three occupied cages sat an alien transport box. The boxes had been salvaged from one of the few alien spaceships shot down by NORAD before meteors pummelled the U.S. emergency capitol into rubble. The eight foot tall, coppery boxes hummed softly. It appeared to be the way most aliens came to Earth and the way most seemed to be packaged for return trips from Earth as well.

When the two specified aliens were secured, Weiss watched as Falconni's men pushed their neuter captives into the centre of the dry pool to join the dozen or so others huddled at the lowest point.

Falconni's was the last team. He led his team out of the pool and up into the flanking bleachers where five other teams waited patiently with most of the nearly two hundred survivors left from the D.C. area group.

Weiss climbed up onto the high dive board. When he had everyone's attention, he said, "You've all done a good job acquiring test subjects. Now, we'll see if my efforts have been equally successful."

He fished a remote control from the front of his lab coat and pressed a button. The transport boxes in each cage hissed open.

"I've developed a mutation of the virus the aliens spread across the Earth to initiate the Zombie Plague. Tests prove direct injection of this new virus will turn any alien into a zombie and its bite will infect other aliens as well." As Weiss spoke, the aliens in their transport boxes shuffled stiffly out, as normal new arrivals did. They looked around and displayed different kinds of surprised reactions. Each of the three transport boxes held a different gender of alien.

"Direct injection is slow and it would be too easy for the aliens to isolate the infected. What I'm testing here is an aerosol version we sprayed on the aliens before we put them in the transport boxes. This test will show if the virus will survive stasis."

The newly released aliens rattled the doors of their cages, some attempted to free their secured fellows. After about twenty minutes, the female and neuter from the transport boxes began to stagger drunkenly before sinking to the floor.

"Just stay with me," Dr. Weiss said to the restless human audience, as he clicked a stopwatch. "We'll know soon. I must say I'm disappointed the virus doesn't seem to affect our male test subject."

In their respective cages, the sick female and neuter coughed and moaned before going still and silent.

Weiss felt his hair stand on end. Even though they were aliens, he recognised the post-death twitches in the female and neuter. Judging by the racket made by the aliens trapped in the cages with the slowly reviving corpses, the doomed aliens knew those signs as well.

Weiss watched the slaughter that followed, and enjoyed it thoroughly. The zombie female and zombie neuter fed on the aliens bound to benches or posts. Within minutes of their gruesome deaths, the mangled victims also tried to get up and feed. A few zombie aliens managed to force open their cages and swarmed over the shrilly screaming neuters at the bottom of the dry pool.

By the end of the hour, only the aliens in the cage where the transport boxes held the infected male were still alive. The neuters in that cage had started coughing as if they'd been infected as well.

"Gentlemen," said Weiss, before nodding to Claire and the trio of female lab workers near her, "and Ladies, it seems we have a success. If Fergusson's and Washington's teams will help with the cleanup here, I have some requisition lists for the rest of you. In five days, I'd like to launch rockets to dispense this virus over the alien space port outside D.C."

Colbert gave Weiss a grin and a thumbs-up, waving two of his techs over to him and pulling out his ever-present notepad.

While a slight majority of the witnesses avidly watched the slaughter below, nearly a third looked sickened. Ms. Karsten wouldn't meet Weiss's eyes.

"No," he thought, "I won't allow their squeamishness to stop me now. I'm going to make the aliens suffer for what they did to Emma, and all of humanity."

"People, listen to me," he shouted until every human eye turned to him. "The aliens landed reinforcements and more colonists last week. If they continue on the same schedule as from the past year, those transport ships will leave in five days, presumably to return to their homeworld. It's important we spread the new virus to the alien homeworld before they realise we've developed this mutation. The only way we can reclaim the Earth or even survive is if we destroy or cripple the invaders at their source."

Weiss turned to watch the mass of alien zombies clawing at the cage of the only living aliens. It was so much like those first horrible days of the Zombie Plague. Back when his Emma ... he shook off the threatening tears and felt cold satisfaction that his theory proved out. The aliens had brought this upon themselves. They turned the Earth into a cannibalistic nightmare, so they deserved the chance to see their world die as well.

"Fuckin' A," Falconni shouted along with the other men cheering Weiss. "That's right Doc. Let's share the love."

"That's the last one," Givens told Falconni as the seven foot long rocket roared into the night. All but one of his team's simple, solid fuel rockets had worked as Colbert's tech had promised.

"None too soon," answered Falconni. "With enough time, even Stick gunners can figure out where we're at." Another green beam punched through the brick wall they hid behind. The beam continued through the cart holding the single rail they'd used as a launcher.

He took a second to watch other small rockets sailing over the alien complex like huge sparklers arcing through the sky. A few had explosive warheads to stir things up, but most sprayed their deadly cargo before hitting the ground. Dr. Weiss estimated if ten percent of the aliens in the complex were infected, it should be enough.

"Let's go pay them a visit," Falconni said before hopping up on top of the four foot wall. The metal and plastic shapes of long untouched playground equipment dotted the park behind him, eerie shadows reaching out in the moonlight. Falconni took a moment to fantasise alien cities looking as dead as this, soon.

He felt uncomfortable out there, at night. The others would as well. It was too easy to miss a lurking zombie and it took only one unlucky second and you were dead. Or worse.

Knowing humans rightly feared moving at night, the alien complex's night time defences concentrated on perimeter defence against zombies. Only two of the rockets fired were hit by alien beam weapons and those were near the end of the bombardment. The unprepared alien counter-battery efforts justified the risk of a night attack.

"I don't like this part of the plan," said Alex. "We've sprayed them like bugs, why do we have to risk getting shot?"

The others mumbled agreement, but grabbed their weapons and filed through the nearby gate anyway.

"Dr. Weiss doesn't want to give them time to figure out what the rockets carried. Aliens rattle pretty easily, so an attack should keep them nice and distracted. We want them to rush off some emergency escape ships and get every plane at Dulles moving out and spread the virus fast," said Falconni, repeating the plan the way it had been explained to him.

"Yeah," drawled Givens, "git some bullets flyin' around an' the big boys'll grab the first ride outta town. D.C. was always that way."

"Well, we couldn't spray all of the alien complexes. Dr. Weiss had the, um, recipe for making the mutant virus radioed to those labs left in Russia, Japan and Cairo. They're supposed to spray it if they can copy his process, but we don't know if they'll be able to. Anyway, we'll need the aliens to carry the virus to their colonies where there aren't people around anymore. The planes they use to evacuate their civilians from here and bring back troops from other complexes should do just fine for spreading the plague."

The men bunched up in the middle of the street, watching dark doorways and broken windows for signs of movement. Falconni hopped down and led the way to their goal — a tall apartment building overlooking the east side of the alien complex.

They trotted the mile and a half to the apartment building, seeing no signs of life more threatening than rats, feral cats and swaying trees. It was almost intoxicating, being out at night and not being attacked.

"Stay frosty, guys," said Hugo, "this'd be a really stupid time to get bit 'cause you're not paying attention."

The euphoria of being out, taunting their fear of the dark, went away when they reached the apartment building.

The Royal stood fifteen stories tall. Broken glass and ruined furniture littered the area immediately around it.

Falconni took a deep breath, trying to silence the voice in his head screaming that the building could be a deathtrap.

"Lights," he said, switching on his own flashlight. This night's missions would see the end of their stockpiled batteries. "Slow and careful. We're going straight to the roof, lots of room up there. Shouldn't be any zombies left in this part of town, but let's do this by the numbers."

It was a nerve-wracking ten minutes, climbing the stairwell to the top. The exterior fire escape looked too badly rusted to even consider using. They found piles of clothes, gnawed bones and other evidence of zombie feasts, but those were years old.

The view from the roof almost made the climb worth the damage to Falconni's nerves. The alien complex was in chaos. Several fires blazed out of control and bright green beams flashed in all directions.

The roughly six mile circle of confiscated buildings and Dulles airport was surrounded by a flattened zone five hundred feet wide with an eight foot, razorwire-topped fence behind it. An ideal fortification to fend off zombies, if folks aren't dropping things on you from space.

A string of human-made, alien-flown aircraft lined up at the airport, one taking off every two minutes or so. As he watched, a huge cigar-shaped spaceship lifted on shimmering orange beams.

"There ya go, boys," Falconni said with a chuckle, "they're taking a nice bellyful of Doc Weiss's bugs back to their homes and families."

"Yeah, good luck with that," Hugo said as he gave a one-finger salute to the fleeing ship.

"We've got some work now, boys," said Falconni, setting up his deer rifle and mounting its scope. Beside him, Givens and Hugo pulled out their long range guns as well. "Keep an eye on our backs, Alex. I'd hate to be disturbed."

Through his 10x scope, Falconni got a good view of the well-lighted complex. Deadly green beams bored through the targets of panicked alien soldiers as well as everything else for a mile or more behind the target. Like the first night of humanity's zombie plague, friendly fire was as much a risk to the aliens as the rapidly multiplying zombies.

"And now for some unfriendly fire to liven things up a bit," Falconni whispered as he spotted a Stick reaction team who seemed to have their act together. Five Sticks rode in a topless Jeep, a pair of M-16s mounted on the roll bar. The squad leader held a quartz beam light and scanned the streets, directing fire on shuffling, blood-spattered alien zombies as well as motioning fleeing civilians to safety.

Falconni's first shot took most of the driver's head in a spray of blue blood. His next proved to be a gut shot for the squad leader. The confused crew didn't see the bleeding Cow staggering from behind a garage until she jumped on them.

He swept his scope around for the next target. He spotted a Bull standing on a concrete bench. The alien took careful aim with a small beam weapon and shot a hole through the head of a bloody, one-armed Stick pushing against a fence gate. Behind the fence, a dozen or more Cows huddled, seemingly catatonic. More dead Sticks stumbled over to push at the gate, ignoring their re-killed brother.

Falconni shot the Bull on the bench. It must have made a sound, drawing the attention of one of the zombie aliens. The wounded Bull fumbled with its dropped and clearly ruined weapon as the zombie drew near.

It took two shots for Falconni to weaken the fence gate enough for the other zombies to force it open. He didn't watch after they pushed through the gate and went for the doomed Cows.

He continued his visual sweep of the complex, looking for signs of effective defence. He didn't bother shooting at fleeing alien civilians, although the steady stream of obscene comments he heard from Givens sounded like the D.C. native didn't care what he shot. In the end, neither did Falconni as long as the target had blue skin.

After an hour of this, Falconni had to have his men shift

positions between shots. Alien gunners figured out they were taking fire and began firing at the apartment building. Alien counter-fire slowed things down, but didn't seem dangerous until Hugo was hit in the shoulder by a high-powered bullet. Falconni assumed it had been fired by an alien, but couldn't be sure.

Alex patched the boy up, while Falconni and Givens alternated looking for shots inside the alien complex with scanning nearby high-rises for other threats.

It was nearly dawn before Falconni had fired down to his last few rounds. He still had his pistol, but shooting himself dry went against every instinct.

Per instructions, he keyed his 60's-vintage walky-talky, "Dr. Weiss, this is Team Baker. It looks like it's pretty much over on the east side of the airport."

"Very good, Team Baker. I have similar reports from the south and west." Weiss's voice sounded odd. Not tired, and certainly not as jazzed as Falconni expected. The doctor had a real hard-on for the aliens since that meteor strike on the hospital. He'd finally joined the rest of the human race on that score.

"Team Baker, observe the base perimeter. Report if you see anything unusual. Weiss out."

Falconni ordered Alex to help Hugo down to the street and then swept his scope across the flattened area outside the complex. He doubted there would be many alien zombies finding their way past the fence, but a live alien might be desperate enough to try his luck outside.

His shoulder ached and his eyes burned, but Falconni was thorough by nature.

Movement caught his eye, something smaller than an alien, even one of their hatchlings or cubs or whatever. A black and white dog limped on three legs across the open ground.

Two fat rats were right on top of it and attacked the injured, feral canine.

"What in hell?" Falconni whispered as the three animals got into a sharp-fanged ball of fur. Why would rats go after a skinny dog like that when they had an alien smorgasbord on the other side of the fence?

He adjusted the magnification of his scope for a better look. The two rats were covered in pale blue alien blood. They had already helped themselves to a snack, but they bore the injured dog down and killed it.

"Somethin' squirrelly is goin' on." Falconni felt a chill run over him like a bucket of ice water as he grabbed blindly for the walky-talky. He watched the attacking rats waddle back towards the complex after they finished chewing on their canine enemy.

After about a minute, the savaged black and white-furred body twitched.

Weiss felt numb as he heard Falconni's report. It came in right after similar reports from the north and south teams.

"I don't know what else t' tell ya, Doc." Falconni's voice sounded grim through the static. "Your new zombie bug works too well. I hope you're happy."

"Understood. Return to base," answered Weiss.

"We'll be back in about an hour. We have one wounded man and..." Weiss heard indistinct shouting and gunfire over the open line, and then Falconni's voice, distant from the radio. "Givens, get back up here. You can't do anything for them now. See if you can block the roof access." Then, the signal was lost.

Weiss heard laughter in his head. It was the laughter of a Devil he did not believe in. Humanity had probably lost the battle against extermination by the aliens, but he and he alone had doomed every living creature on Earth. Sharing that fate with the alien homeworld wouldn't help those few humans who'd survived so much misery. It wouldn't bring back Emma. It wouldn't bring back their daughter.

Shouts echoed down the hallway outside his lab. He heard the hysterical squeal of Davis's voice through the babel. They would come for him soon, not that it would matter.

Weiss could have made that mutation over a year ago, but knew there were risks. It took his personal loss to make him take his deal with the Devil. His selfishness alone had written the end for humanity, not something he could blame on the aliens.

Someone pounded on the lab door. It was time to pay the Piper.

# THE LUCKY PENNY

TIM JEFFREYS

Alfie couldn't help thinking he was too late. He was sweating and out of breath when he burst into the bedroom. He had already pictured the scene as he hurried up the stairs: the family members clustered around the bed; his mother sat at the foot weeping; his father in the bed, eyes closed, his hands folded on his chest, his face blank and restful. *It's too late*, someone would say. *You're too late, Alfie, he's gone.*

Instead, to his surprise, he discovered his father alone and propped up on pillows in the luxurious four-poster. His face did look calm and restful but his eyes were open. They turned on Alfie when he entered the room.

Halting, Alfie said almost in anger, "Pops?"

His father gazed back at him for a moment, then smiled. "Son."

"What the hell's this?" said Alfie. "Do you know how hard I put my foot down to get here so quickly? Mother rang and said you were at death's door. Do you think its easy travelling half way across the country on New Year's Eve?"

The old man continued to gaze at him, still smiling, as if

he hadn't noticed his son's anger. Alfie could see the change in his father's face more clearly now. He had not noticed before, not consciously, but his father's face had always been shadowed with anxiety, even in the happiest times and despite everything, despite all the wealth. Now the shadow was gone. When his father spoke, his voice was calm.

"I've warned you before about speeding in that car. I never should have bought you a sports car. It's too much for you. A car like that, you have to respect. If you don't, you'll finish up..."

"Never mind that," said Alfie. "Why was I summoned here when you're clearly not dying? Why did mother make out that you were?"

His father's eyes shifted towards the window at his side, which looked out across the grounds of the house. The lawns had a blanket of clean, undisturbed snow which glistened in the morning sunlight. Beside the window was a grandfather clock. The old man stared at it. It showed the time as twenty past eleven.

"Because I told her too."

"Why?"

"Because today's the day."

"The day for what?"

"Today's the day I'm going to die."

Alfie felt his anger dissipate. "Pops," he said, sighing. "How could you know that? The doctors said you're..."

The old man looked at his son again. Alfie could see the certainty in his eyes.

"Because I know. I've always known."

"Don't be ridiculous. How could you?"

"Sit down, son," the old man said, gesturing at the chair beside the bed. "Have you come alone?"

"Who should I have come with?"

"Why, that lovely girl. What was her name?"

"If you mean Sofia, that's over."

"Oh. Well, what about work?"

Alfie fell into the chair next to the bed, sighing. "There isn't any. I had to liquidate the business. It just wasn't performing. Actually, I was going to ask if I could borrow some money."

"I see. I thought there was something wrong. You're just not lucky, son. You remind me of my father. Your grandfather. He wasn't always rich and successful. Early in his life he had terrible luck. Just terrible."

"Is that so? Well, he must have managed to turn it around at some point. What changed?"

The old man's eyes shifted now to a desk on the opposite side of the room. "I've got something for you. That's if you want it. I had your mother fetch it from my safety deposit box at the bank last Christmas. It's been here all this time. Over there. Top drawer."

Alfie got up and went to the desk. "What am I looking for?"

"It's in a small blue box. Bring it here. Don't open it."

Alfie brought the blue box to his father and placed it beside him on the sheets.

"You didn't know this, son, but your grandfather was reduced to begging when he was a young man. They were hard times after the war. He couldn't even afford to feed himself. Then one day someone tossed him a penny. An old George Fifth penny. And the strange thing about it, at least for your grandfather, was the year on it. It just happened to be the same year your grandfather was born."

"So what?" said Alfie. "A coincidence. He kept it, I suppose?"

"Oh yes, he kept it. He said it was his lucky penny. And his luck did change after that. Everything came easy to him in the end — money, fame, women, good health. He died a very rich and happy man. Just as I will. I've had a good life."

"Don't say that, Pops. There's plenty of life in you still. You'll be singing Auld Lang Syne and sipping champagne with the rest of us come midnight."

The old man looked thoughtful for a moment, his eyes clouding. Again, he shifted his gaze towards the grandfather clock. Then he went on, "He gave his lucky penny to me before he died. He wanted me to have all the luck that he'd enjoyed."

"But, Pops, you don't honestly believe he got lucky because of the penny? You make your own luck in this world."

"Perhaps," the old man said, and then a fit of coughing overcame him. Concerned, Alfie got up and stood over his father. One of the old man's hands gestured towards a jug of water on the bedside table. Alfie filled a glass and held it to his father's lips.

"Looks like my luck's just about run out," the old man said, with a rueful smile.

"I told you not to talk like that. The doctors are optimistic."

"Doctors only tell you want they think you want to hear. There's something else, see, about your grandfather's story. One side of the penny had the year of his birth on it, but on the other side was a different year. 1981, the year he died. He didn't make the connection until he got ill of course. He knew he was going to die that year. The penny told him. Two days before he passed away, he gave the penny to me."

Alfie couldn't help but laugh. "That's absurd."

The old man stared at him, mild outrage in his eyes. "It's true! It's all true!"

"Well, say it's true. What has that got to do with you?"

"Because when I took the penny, the years changed. It was the year of *my* birth on the one side with George Fifth. And on the other — this year! This year that's about to be over! I've lived my whole life knowing the year of my death. That was the price of all the luck."

"I don't believe you," Alfie said, reaching for the little box which he presumed contained the magic penny—

"Don't touch it!" his father shouted. "Not yet. Give it to me. I'll show it to you."

Alfie handed the box to his father and the old man lifted the lid. He held the opened box out for Alfie to see. Inside was a small discoloured copper penny, on which was the profile of a man with a large moustache. Leaning closer, Alfie could just make out the writing on the coin. Around the top half was an inscription in Latin. At the bottom was inscribed a year.

"That is strange," he said. "Why would a George Fifth penny have this year printed on it? Maybe it was a misprint."

"It's no misprint. On the other side it has my birth year."

"Let me see."

"No, don't touch it! Don't touch it yet! You have to think first if you really want it. Think about the price!"

Alfie glanced up and met his father's eyes. "So now you're going to give this penny to me, if I say I want it, just like you're father gave it to you. And presumably I'll have all the luck and money and women that anyone could ever want."

"Yes, but you have to understand there's a price. The

dates will change, once you accept it."

Alfie smiled. *The old man's gone senile*, he thought. *Probably best just to humour him.* "What if I just turned it over and didn't look at that side ever again."

"You'll look. Eventually, you'll look."

The old man was about to turn the coin over for Alfie to see the other side when he was seized by a bout of coughing again, stronger this time. Alfie reached for the water, but his father couldn't drink it. The coughing had a hold of him.

"I'll get mother. And the doctor!" said Alfie, and rushed out of the room.

Alfie waited outside the room whilst the doctor attended to his father. Eventually, his mother emerged and said, "Your father needs rest."

"And I need a drink."

Alfie went alone to the silent lounge and poured scotch from his father's decanter. He sat and stared at the Christmas tree for a while, remembering Christmases he had spent as a child. Always so many presents. Always so much food. The family had never wanted for anything.

*And all thanks to a lucky penny*, he thought, smiling to himself.

He got up and poured another glass of scotch. In no time he had emptied the decanter.

Around three o'clock, his mother came into the room looking teary but composed. Alfie sat up straight.

"Darling," she said. "Your father, he's gone. He just never woke up."

*"What?"*

Alfie poured himself a final drink and sat looking out of the open door towards the stairway that led upstairs. He finished his drink and made his way up to his father's bedroom once more.

His father's face was changed now in a way he could never have imagined. It looked empty and cold, like a shell. Whatever had been of his father was gone. Noticing the little blue box on the bedside table, Alfie picked it up and opened it.

"I guess you were right, Pops, it does say this year. Another few hours and you would have been clear, but I guess it was your time, huh? All year you've been waiting for it."

Now a few tears came, more at the thought of his father spending a year anticipating his own death than the fact that he was now gone.

"You old fool," he said. Without thinking, he plucked the penny from the box and flipped it over. He wanted to see if the year of his father's birth was really printed on the other side. He wasn't sure of the year, he would have to check with his mother later, but he wanted to see what year was on the coin anyway.

"Huh?"

He stared at the penny.

On the back, along with a royal coat of arms and another Latin inscription was indeed printed a different year from the front, but not one Alfie had expected.

"That can't be right."

He glanced at his father's still face, then around the room, but there was no one to confirm what he was seeing.

"That's the year *I* was born."

And what was on the other side now? Alfie remembered his father saying, *You'll look. Eventually, you'll look.*

*No, I won't!* Alfie thought. He put the lid back on the box and stuffed it into his jacket pocket. *I don't want to know!*

He hadn't even reached the door of the room before he took the box out and opened it again.

It still had the year of his birth on it, right there under George Fifth.

*It's no good! I can't stand not knowing! I'll have to see! I'll have to look!*

Before he could stop himself, he turned the coin over.

"No!" he shouted. "That's wrong!"

He moved back towards the bed, but then he remembered that his father was gone. He stared at the coin, flipping it over. On one side, instead of the year of his father's birth was written the year of his — Alfie's — birth, but the other side hadn't changed from when his father had first showed it to him.

His eyes moved towards the grandfather clock by the window. It was almost six. It was still some hours until midnight, but already in his head he could hear the strains of Old Lang Syne.

He flung the penny and its box to the floor.

He ran from the room, ran down the stairs and out of the house. He ran to the driveway where his car was parked, scrabbling in his pockets for the keys. He had to get away, drive away.

Nothing could happen to him if he just kept driving.

# WHITE LINES, WHITE CROSSES

## ANDREW J MCKIERNAN

Just off the highway on the main road into town, some douche has wrapped his car around a tree. Traffic is backed up ten deep and the red and blue lights of emergency vehicles strobe the night.

Ryan leans forward in the back seat, trying to catch a glimpse of the wreckage, but already his father is inching their car onto the opposite verge. Two police cars and an ambulance block most of the road and a blue tarpaulin has been strung up to prevent anyone seeing more than the rear bumper of a white Commodore sedan and the P-plate pasted to its back window. Two black lines of tyre rubber twist and curve like serpents across the asphalt, crossing and recrossing the white centre line, describing the vehicle's final trajectory.

"You two stay here," his father says as their car pulls to a stop. His mother puts a hand onto his father's knee, concern written all over her face. Ryan knows what his mother is thinking. They haven't even arrived in the town yet, haven't seen their new home, and his father isn't supposed to start work until Monday.

"You know I've got to, Marion," his father says. "It's my

job. I can't just drive on." And then the door is open and he's out, slamming the door closed behind him and rushing off into the night.

Ryan and his mother sit in the car and wait. The windows are wound up against the cold and some uncool band from the 80s is playing on the radio. His iPod battery is flat after the three hour drive. He wishes he'd charged it before they left so he could listen to something that wasn't recorded before he was born. He stares out the window, bored and arse-numb from sitting so long, just wanting this trip to be over.

That is when he sees the first of them. A small white cross nailed to a tree on the roadside. The tree's trunk is carved with initials and hearts. Around its base are scattered bunches of dead or dying flowers, beer cans and an old stuffed teddy bear. Something has been written on the cross in black but Ryan can't read most of it. All he can make out are the letters R.I.P. in chunky block-letters.

There are more, too. Ryan turns back to the scene of the accident and sees a tree and a telegraph pole both sporting crosses. One is little more than two sticks tied together and painted white. The other is more elaborate, cut from a single piece of wood with detailed curves adorning the cross arms. He leans forward and looks over his mother's shoulder and out the front windscreen. Three, four, five. Maybe six of them. Every third or fourth tree and telegraph pole carries one and he can see no more as the road into town disappears in the darkness.

The car door opens, startling Ryan and his mother both. His father is standing there, blood all over his shirt and pants. His face is pale and his sparse hair slicked back with sweat. He doesn't say a word as he slumps into the driver's seat and starts the engine and pulls the car back onto the road. Over by the accident, paramedics are loading a sheet covered trolley into the back of the ambulance.

Their car moves on and continues its journey the final ten kilometres into their new town. Their new home. Ryan's father's new job. No one speaks a word and even the radio has fallen quiet. Ryan counts the crosses that line the roadside. Twenty at least. Each cross surrounded by flowers and photos and empty beer cans like offerings at an altar.

"Hey! You're Ryan, yeah? New up from Sydney?"

Ryan turns and the strap of his backpack slips from his shoulder. He grabs the bag before it can hit the floor and looks into the face of a boy he's seen walking the asphalt quadrangle with a posse of hangers-on. The boy isn't in any of Ryan's classes but a few of his 'gang' are. Loud mouthed smartarses, mostly.

"Yeah, that's right."

"Must be boring for ya out here. No beaches. No cinemas. Even the video shop's crap. I'm Trent."

Trent holds out his hand and Ryan stares at it for a moment before offering his own and they shake. Trent's grip is tight and his hand only moves up and down once — a short and sharp flick of his arm — before letting go.

"Never been into the beach much anyways," Ryan says. "So, what does everyone 'round here do for fun?"

"You got your licence?"

"Yeah, on my 'P's."

"Well, shit man! You're in business. Got your own car?"

"Nah, just my Dad's."

"He the new doctor over the hospital?"

"Yeah."

"Should give you plenty of chances while he's on shift then."

"Chances for what?"

"Hoonin' bro! That's 'bout all we got to do 'round here. We take our cars down the paddock on weekends and just do some laps. Burn-outs and doughnuts. You'll be in, won't ya?"

Ryan isn't sure. He knows his father wouldn't like it. But Trent doesn't seem too bad. And what else is he going to do? This town doesn't even have a library, and he can forget all about decent broadband. No more late-night zombiefests over the Xbox with his mates. His *old* mates, he reminds himself. They're three hundred kilometres away now. In this town, three hundred kilometres seems more like three hundred years, his friends now living in some far off future. And then there's his father's car. A 2008 Lexus GS300 with a 3.0 litre V6 engine that his father brags can do 0 to 100 in seven seconds and a top speed of 250 K's per hour. It might be something to test out those claims.

"Yeah, okay. I'm in, I guess," Ryan says and Trent smiles.

"Good man, good man. I think you're going to fit in just fine. You should start hangin' out with us at lunch. Whatdya reckon?"

Ryan shrugs and then nods. Why not? He doesn't really know anyone else.

"Cool. Meet you out back of E-block."

And then Trent is walking away, head held high and a cocksure swagger in his step.

"We gonna go visit Pete tonight?"

"Depends if anyone's got any beers," Trent says, a cigarette hanging from his mouth.

"My old man just filled the fridge in the garage. Reckon the old fuck won't miss any. He's too pissed to count most the time." This is from some guy named Boof. As in boofhead. He looks pretty pleased that he's the one to offer up his dad's grog to the group.

They're sitting out the back of E-block. About seven or eight of them, all clustered around Trent who sits above them on an aluminium bench like some teenage messiah. Ryan stands back a bit, not sure if he'll be accepted as one of them. Not yet sure if he wants to be.

"Wonder if Pete saw 'em?" someone asks and they all shrug.

"Only Pete'd know that," Trent says. "And he ain't talkin' much at the moment. We'll go see him tonight though. You comin', Ryan?"

"Umm ... who's Pete?"

"Mate of ours. Died last weekend in an accident. Gonna go out by the tree he hit and have a drink with him. You in?"

It's a Thursday and Ryan's not sure if he'll be allowed out on a school night, but he says yes anyway. He doesn't know why. To try and make some friends, he guesses. Almost a week and he still barely knows anyone at school. He's just too different to most of them. Like a foreigner.

"Cool," Trent says. "There's a wreckers over on Murphy Street, right down the end. Meet us there around seven and I'll give you a lift."

Ryan and his mum fight for the first time in months. She doesn't want him going out after dinner on a school night. He doesn't want to be the weird kid from the city for the rest of his life. He's done all his homework. All his chores. He'll be home before ten thirty — which is his normal bedtime anyway — and there is no damn reason why he can't go out. He's seventeen now, not ten. When is she going to let him grow up?

"It's not that, Ryan. I know you're seventeen. But I don't know these boys."

"I don't know them either yet, Mum. I don't know *anyone* here!"

"We haven't even been here a week. Give it a chance. You'll make friends soon enough."

"Dad would let me go out. You still treat me like a baby."

And there it is, he's played the parent vs parent card. Ryan knows that it will either soften her up or escalate the situation to an entirely new level. But he's feeling lost and lonely and not at all in a mood to give in.

"Your father's not here, is he? I am."

"Yeah, well, he's *never* here."

"That's not fair, Ryan. Look, I know you're lonely, but—"

"No! None of it's fair, Mum! Dad always working. Us moving. Leaving all my friends. Not allowed to make new ones. You keeping me locked up. You're the lonely one with no friends. No wonder. You're such a bitch!"

It's out of his mouth before he even realises he's said it. There is shock on his mother's face, and that look of disappointment he so rarely sees. A look that makes him feel small and childish.

"That's it, Ryan! You. Will. Not. Speak to me like that. Go to your room. Now! I'm not dealing with this. Your father can speak to you when he gets home."

Ryan turns and stalks from the room, as tall and gangly as a seventeen year old boy can be. His hand flicks out in anger — more at himself than at his mother — and sweeps a pile of paperwork from the kitchen bench onto the floor.

"Pick that up right now, Ryan Morrison," his mother yells at his back but he keeps moving down the hall and into his bedroom. He slams the door behind him. Flops onto his bed. Tears well up in his eyes and his throat releases an anguished sob.

Already he's regretting the words he has said. Cheap shots. He knows his mother wasn't happy about moving here either. He heard them arguing on and off in the weeks leading up to the move, late at night when they thought he was asleep. She's lost just as many friends as he has. No more twice weekly gym visits. No more Book Club or Chardonnays by the pool. All she'll have here are CWA bake-offs and the occasional visit to the pub beer-garden for a schnitzel. But still...

His hand reaches out in a teenage reflex to stem the silence and turns on his iPod. Music bursts from the dock speakers. Hard and noisy and filled with growling guitars, pounding beats. He bangs his head into his pillow a few times. Not to the beat, but in pure frustration. What will Trent and Boof and all the others think of him now? He said he'd go. Trent will be waiting for him out front of the wreckers. And when he doesn't turn up, the ribbing will begin behind his back. By the time he gets to school in the morning, he'll be the butt of everyone's jokes.

He turns the music up louder, knowing his mother will leave him alone until his father gets home. It is always like this when they fight, this mutual choice to ignore each other. It doesn't happen often but when it does the silence between them is easier. Apologies will have to be made and punishments endured, but not until after his father returns at eleven. Even that depends on what sort of night his father has had at the hospital. If he's had it tough, if he's too tired, it will wait until morning. But Ryan knows that neither his mother or father will let it go. There *will* be a talking to.

And so, if he's going to be in trouble anyway, what does it matter what he does now? He's already disappointed his mum. Why disappoint his new friends as well?

He gets off the bed. Wipes his eyes with his sleeve. The window is already partly open and it doesn't take much to slide it further and climb out into the night.

Nobody is waiting outside the wreckers when he arrives. He's only five minutes late. A couple of cars are parked in the street but they're empty of people, windows wound down, cigarette packets and empty beer cans littering their floors. He walks up and down the length of the wrecking yard's fence a few times. Stops outside its high iron gates. Keeps an eye on the road for incoming headlights. Sits on the gutter and waits a little longer.

He's beginning to think he's come out here for nothing. Risked further dispute with his parents. This is something he would never have done a week ago. He feels as childish as he suspects his mother thinks he is, and a little bit stupid too. Trent was probably never even here. They're probably all out somewhere, drinking and smoking and laughing at the city boy. He kicks a rusting piece of metal with his foot and it skitters and spins across the road.

"Hey, you gonna sit there playin' football with that thing all night? Or ya comin' in to join us?"

Ryan jumps at the sound of the voice and turns. It's Trent, face peeking out from a hole in the chainlink fence.

Away from the streetlights, the interior of the wrecking yard is dark, illuminated only by a sliver of moon set about by clouds. Under this pale light, Trent guides Ryan through a maze of twisted and rusting vehicles. He says nothing as they walk. Somewhere up ahead, Ryan can hear voices and music playing as if from an old, tinny radio. Glass crunches beneath their feet. Trent lights a cigarette and the tiny flame from his lighter flares across chrome bumper bars and the grill badges of Holdens and Fords, Mazdas and Subarus. The cars are stacked three or four high and the shadows of cats move through them and leap between them.

"Where we going?" Ryan asks and Trent grunts.

They thread their way through a canyon of cars. Emerge into a clearing ringed by piles of hub-caps and stacks of engine parts. The headlights of an old VW beetle light the circle and distorted heavy metal pounds from its stereo speakers. In the centre, a small fire burns inside the concavity of a tyre rim and three boys sit around it, drinking beers and smoking cigarettes. The boys all look up at Trent as he approaches. Ryan follows cautiously. He has no idea what they are all doing here.

"Ho! Look what I found in the gutter. Hey, Stevo, you'd

better of saved us some beers."

Stevo gets up and takes two cans from the green carton that rests beside him. He hands one to Trent and the other to Ryan.

Ryan has tasted beer a few times before, but never more than a sip or two. The can isn't quite cold but he pops the top anyway and takes a drink. It is surprisingly good.

Trent drains his beer in two long swallows. Tosses his cigarette butt into the fire and crushes the beer can beneath his heel. He motions for Ryan to follow and heads off slowly towards the far side of the clearing. He grabs another beer from the carton as he passes. Stevo and Boof and the other boy get up from where they're squatting and fall in behind Trent, their steps slow and purposeful. Like a funeral procession. Ryan follows.

At the edge of the clearing rests a white Commodore sedan. Its front end is as crumpled as Trent's beer can. The windscreen is gone. Trent stops when he gets there and waits for the others to catch up and then he squeezes himself into the driver's seat. Stevo and Boof slide into the back. The other boy moves towards the front passenger seat but Trent shakes his head.

"In the back, Grant. I want Ryan to ride shotgun."

Grant climbs into the back with Boof and Stevo. He doesn't look happy about it.

"C'mon man," Trent says. "Hop in. This'll be a trip."

Ryan tries the handle but the door is either locked or jammed shut. Trent reaches over and gives it a hard shove from the inside and the door pops open with a screech of metal on metal. Inside, there isn't much of a front seat left for Ryan to sit in. The steering wheel has been removed on the driver's side but Trent still only has room to sit with both legs hunched, knees under his chin. The passenger side is even worse. The dashboard intrudes into the seat space, overhanging it like a ledge. Small squares of glass are everywhere. Ryan brushes the glass from the passenger seat and slides in sideways, legs exposed to the night.

"See here," Trent says, pointing to the dashboard just above the instrument panel. "Still blood all over the place."

Ryan sees where he's pointing. In the near dark they look like splashes of black ink, and not just confined to the dash either. The upholstered ceiling is mottled with dark specks. The driver's seat is spattered with them and beneath Trent's arse Ryan can see the fabric is a totally different colour from the rest of the car. Even his own seat, he realises, is covered with splashes of darkness.

He remembers the car wrapped around a tree on the night they came to town. The tarpaulin hiding the view. The sheet covered trolley. The blood all over his father's shirt. And suddenly he feels sick. His head spins as he tries to stand up and get out. Bangs his forehead on the door lintel and falls back into the seat.

"Woah, man! Chill a little," Trent says and rests his hand on Ryan's shoulder. The boys in the back are laughing. "It ain't nothin' but dried blood. No need to freak."

Ryan gasps for a breath. His heart is racing. Forehead aching. What are they doing here in this death car?

"This is Pete's car?" he asks between panicked inhalations.

"Yeah, 'course it is. Whole reason we came here. Don't worry though, Pete's not here. He'll be out by his tree on Bundarra Road."

The boys laugh at this too, but Trent ignores them. He points through the empty windscreen.

"Look, see how your side's more smashed up than mine?

He tried to swerve at the last minute. It's a driver's instinct to steer away from the point of impact. Reason why passengers are killed more often than drivers. He must'a been goin' hella fast."

"Yeah, pretty fast," Boof says from the back. "Wonder if he saw 'em?"

"Dunno." Trent finishes his beer and tosses it out the window. "Maybe we should go ask? Pete's probably dyin' for a beer and a ciggie anyways."

Everyone except Ryan bursts into gales of laughter.

Trees and telegraph poles fly by so fast they're a blur. There are no streetlights and the moon has disappeared behind the hills. The car's halogen headlights cut through the oncoming darkness like frozen lightning, but it's not enough for Ryan. The road has too many curves. Too many dips and crests. There never seems to be enough asphalt to light up. Everything is a blind corner or hidden bend until the last instant.

AC/DC is playing on the stereo and Trent is singing along. No, he's shouting, with no thought at all for the melody. Not that AC/DC ever had much thought for melody either in Ryan's opinion. He'd rather be listening to Hilltop Hoods or Bliss n Eso but he doubts Trent has even heard of them. He plants his feet hard and grasps the edge of his seat with both hands. His knuckles and face are white. He tries not to swear or say a word as Trent pushes the car around another bend. Tyres squeal hot rubber across the road.

Two other cars follow not far behind. Stevo and Boof are

in Stevo's dad's ute; a working man's vehicle if ever there was one, bullbar on the front and tool-locker in the back. Grant drives his own 1996 Toyota Corolla. This is the sort of vehicle Ryan would have called a Granny-car back in the city, but Grant has made the sort of modifications that would scare anyone's grandmother. According to Grant, it's been lowered so much the wheel arches near scrape the low profile tyres and 17" mag wheels. He's dropped in a 1.8 litre turbo-charged twin-cam engine to replace the stock 1.6 litre. Added a 3" exhaust and extractors. New racing seats and a Ghepardo steering wheel. Ryan was told all this as they were leaving the wrecking yard, but he barely understood a word of it.

"There's a legend about Bundarra Road," Trent shouts above the music. "Back in the early 80s some kid was driving along here in his Torana. Five of his friends crammed in like sardines in a can. Lost control on a bend and that was it. Hit a telegraph pole and ripped the car in two. All six dead. Just like that."

Trent looks across at Ryan and Ryan just wishes he'd keep his eyes on the road.

"Legend is, if you drive along here fast enough, you'll see 'em. All six of 'em. Just standin' there on the side of the road. All bloody and twisted like."

"Have you seen them?" Ryan asks.

"Not yet, I ain't."

"What happens if you do?"

"Then you're already good as dead. Nobody who's seen 'em has ever lived."

Ryan looks out the window at the rapidly passing landscape. He thinks he can see flashes of white. The crosses set along the roadside that he saw on the drive into town.

"If no one who's seen 'em ever lived, how did the story start in the first place?"

Trent frowns at the question, shifts down gear on the upgrade and guns the engine. The car leaps forward like an untamed horse. Ryan is thrown back, head colliding hard against the headrest. He clutches his seat even tighter.

A cross has already been erected at the site of Pete's accident. Two pieces of four-by-two, crossed and nailed at the centre and painted white. It has been planted in the ground at the foot of the tree. Upon it is written:

*Peter Alan Wakely*
*1995–2012*
*Always in Our Hearts*

Someone has placed a bunch of fresh flowers at the base of the cross. A couple of sympathy cards too, already fading like memories. Tied around the trunk of the tree is a school football jersey. A photograph has been nailed to the bark beneath it; bark still scarred and streaked with white paint from the car's final impact.

"Here's to you, Pete," Trent says and pours a can of beer onto the ground before the cross. The earth drinks up the amber liquid. Trent lights a cigarette, takes a deep puff and sticks it in the dirt, butt down. "Have a cig too, mate. You've earned it."

The other boys nod. They're hunkered down around the cross and the tree. None of them say a word. Ryan sits with them but feels very much apart. He isn't one of them. He never knew Peter Alan Wakely. He gets up and walks over to the tree. Looks at the photo. It's a blow-up of a class photo. Pete in his pale-blue collared school shirt, hair short but tussled on top. Face slightly freckled and smiling. He looks just like any other kid. Ryan wonders why there were no announcements, no services, at school. Back in the city this would have been in the papers and probably on the news. There would have been announcements and memorial assemblies and possibly even a day off. Counsellors made available to distressed students.

He turns and asks, "Hey? Did you all go to the funeral?"

The four boys look up at him like this is the oddest question anyone could ever have asked.

"Nah. Why?"

"I just thought, well … you know. It was his funeral. Family and friends saying goodbye and all that."

They're still looking at him strangely. A silence accompanies their gaze that he feels an urgent need to fill.

"And, you know, I was thinking. If you wanted to have a beer with Pete, why not at his grave or whatever?"

Boof and Stevo and Grant, they all turn to Trent. It seems natural for them to defer to him. As if they have nothing to say of their own unless Trent hasn't voiced it first.

"What's the point? All you'll find at the cemetery is a bag of rotting flesh and bone. Probably not even that. Just a plaque and an urn of ashes. Pete ain't there. He's here. This is his spot. Can't you feel him here? With us?"

Ryan *is* starting to feel something. He thinks of that feeling as 'creeped out'. Creeped out by the four boys crouched in front of a cross like a congregation before an altar. Creeped out by them talking about a dead friend like he's right there with them. Instead of answering Trent's question, he turns and looks back down the road towards town. He can see the crosses that line the roadside. So many of them. They seem to almost glow against the darkness.

A truck is coming down off the highway, headlights blazing. It rounds the bend near Pete's cross. Lights play across the trees and telegraph poles, throwing shadows of branches and leaves and guardrails. And, for just a moment, he sees the outlines of people, the pale faces of the dead, standing mute along the side of the road beside their crosses.

Ryan turns away in an attempt to un-see what he has already seen. The truck's horn blares. Its rear lights wash red across the night as it passes. Ghastly crimson light illuminates the faces of the four boys staring up at him. Smiling at him.

"Look, ummm, I've really got to be heading home. It's pretty late."

Trent looks back at him with what might be sympathy. Or pity. Or contempt.

"Nah, man," Grant says. "It's not even ten o'clock. Still plenty more beers left. Pete's barely got to know you yet."

Trent finishes another beer and rises. He tosses the can off into the bush.

"Sokay, I'll take him home. You guys hang out here a little longer if you want."

They walk back to Trent's car in silence. Ryan has a feeling Trent is pissed at him for wanting to leave. He's still not sure he wants to be friends with these boys, but he doesn't want to be enemies either. They've been good to him. Tried to accept him. Maybe they're just too different to really be friends.

Trent's car is a jet-black Ford Falcon. Not new, but well

maintained and decked out with shiny mags and a blower on the bonnet that probably does nothing except look cool. Ryan wonders what the boys would think of his dad's Lexus. Would they think it was cool? Or would it just be a rich-wanker-from-the-city's car? He's sure it would kick the arse of Trent's or Grant's cars on an open stretch of road though.

Behind them, the other three boys begin to sing, loud and raucous. Ryan doesn't recognise the song.

"That was Pete's favourite," Trent says, beer beginning to slur his words as they climb into the car. Trent starts the engine, revs it a bit, and then spins the car out onto the road.

His father's car isn't in the driveway when Ryan gets home just after ten. He sneaks down the side of the house and back through his bedroom window. The music is still playing. He turns down the volume. Turns off the light and settles onto his bed. He doesn't bother getting changed, just takes off his shoes and socks and throws them into a corner of the room. He lies there for a long while, trying to sleep but seeing only the faces of the people standing by the side of the road. The dead people standing beside their white crosses.

When he next looks at his clock radio it is almost eleven. He switches off his iPod and rolls over. Listens for the sound of his father's car and wonders if the chiding for his earlier behaviour will come tonight or in the morning. He hasn't forgotten the way he spoke to his mother and doubts that she will either. It is something both he and his father will have to deal with eventually. Probably sooner rather than later.

No car pulls up in the driveway. Nobody knocks on his door or enters his room and he finally finds himself drifting off to sleep. In those last moments before the veil falls, Ryan imagines that he can hear sirens screaming along the main road out of town.

He eats his breakfast alone. Porridge and toast. A breakfast of boredom, fitting for the inevitable tedium of the school day ahead. His father must have arrived home late. His car is in the driveway but he's yet to stir from the bedroom. Ryan's mother is in the shower and still not talking to him. Ryan is dressed and waiting to brush his teeth and hair before she emerges from the bathroom.

"Don't disturb your father," she says as they pass each other in the hallway. "He didn't get home until well after midnight."

"Yes, Mum."

"Another accident out on the main road. What is it with people and they way they drive?"

And then she's gone, shaking her head and off into the kitchen. Ryan doesn't have an answer for her anyway. He's too busy thinking about the sirens he thought had been part of a dream.

"Grant's in hospital," is the first thing Trent says to Ryan when he gets to school. "Lost it on Bundarra Road on the way home. Car's trashed. Fuckin' shame. He did a lot of work on that old girl."

"What about Grant? He okay?"

"Nah, don't think so. But he's alive."

"For now," Stevo says, walking up behind them. "My old man towed the car back. Says it's a fuckin' mess."

Ryan thinks of his father working back late to keep Grant alive and all these guys are worried about is the car. The principal makes no announcement at the morning assembly but students do seem to be talking, whispering about what has happened. The most common thing he hears is: "Do you think he saw them?"

"See you tonight, yeah?" Trent calls as school lets out.

"Umm, yeah, sure. See you tonight."

Ryan doesn't head straight home. He turns right when he should turn left and continues on to the hospital. It's a flat, single-storey building very different from the sprawling multi-storey complexes he is used to visiting in the city. The front doors aren't even automatic and the blast of air-conditioning he has prepared himself for as he enters never arrives. The tepid air smells of disinfectant.

A receptionist points him down a long corridor and offers up a room number without question. There is no ICU. No oncology or maternity wards. Just room after room filled with beds. Children laid out as neighbours to the elderly. Injured and infected side by side.

Ryan finds Grant in the far corner of a room lined four beds to a side. The blinds are closed against the afternoon sun, drawing tiger-stripes of light and dark across the bedsheets. Metal stands are hung with bags that leak liquids into his veins. Boxy machines flicker with LEDs and beep in disjointed rhythms. Both his arms are encased in plaster, and from the bulky shapes defined by the rise and fall of the sheets, Ryan suspects Grant's legs are too. His head is wrapped in bandages spotted with blood. Eyes and nose and cheekbones black with bruises. Lips swollen like overripe plums.

Ryan can only stand and stare. He doesn't know what to say to this boy he has only known for a day. Doesn't know if the boy is even awake. Doesn't really understand why he came here in the first place. But then he steps up to the bed and softly speaks the boy's name.

Grant's puffy eyes open to thin slits. He looks around and sees Ryan standing close over him. A thin and pained smile manifests momentarily upon his lips.

"I saw them," he croaks. "I really saw them, man. You saw them too. I know because they told me. You saw them and they saw you."

Machines beep erratically. An alarm goes off. Grant's body shudders under the sheets. His eyes open wide and roll back to whites. Teeth clench tight in a rictus grin. His bottom lip splits. Blood bursts forth and trails down his chin.

Nurses rush in, pushing Ryan out of their way. They're all talking loudly to each other. Issuing orders. Someone calls for a crash cart and Ryan, feeling dazed by what Grant has said, backs into the corridor and turns and walks away.

"I'm sorry about your friend, Ryan. We really did do everything we could."

Ryan nods and forces an accepting shrug. He knows his father is trying to comfort him but it isn't Grant's death that he's worried about.

"I didn't really know him, Dad. Only met him once. I was actually coming to see you but, when I got here, well ... kids were talking at school and, you know, I just thought..."

"It's okay. You're allowed to be upset. That's normal. You're looking pretty pale, bud. Maybe you should sit down a few minutes. Want me to buy you a Coke or something?"

"Yeah, sure. That'd be good."

Ryan sits and waits for his father to return. His shaking has stopped but now he feels wiped out. Drained and hollow. He'd rest if he could but each time he closes his eyes he sees Grant shuddering on the bed, eyes rolling back in their sockets. Or the figures standing by the side of the road. Grant's final words roll around in his mind.

"Here, get this into you. The sugar will help."

His father pushes a cold can into his hand, the top already popped. Ryan takes a long series of swallows.

"Ummm, Dad? Some guys are having a games night tonight and they asked me to go. I was wondering if I could and if, ah, if maybe I could borrow the car to get there and back?"

"Your mother said there was some trouble last night?"

Ryan nods, abashed.

"Have you apologised?"

Ryan nods again, lying. He'll make sure he does as soon as he gets home. In case his father asks. His father stares down at him for a moment, considering.

"I guess it's been a pretty tough week. Doesn't excuse

the way you treated your mother, and we'll still be having a nice long talk before the weekend's through, but I guess that'd be okay. Gotta be back here before eleven to pick me up though? Think you can manage that?"

"Yeah, sure. No problem."

"Okay, I'll talk to your mum and let her know we had a chat. I'll tell her it's all sorted. You okay for me to get back to work?"

"Yeah, Dad. And thanks."

"Just take it easy on your Mum, eh? This move has been hard on her too."

"I will."

"And go easy on the car!"

Ryan accelerates the Lexus out of the bend. The back end doesn't even twitch as he lines up on the straight. He can feel the power of the engine through the soles of his feet. His iPod is plugged into the stereo and 'Definition' by the Resin Dogs pours from the speakers, crystal clear and pumping with bass. His fingers tap out the rhythm on the steering wheel.

Somewhere up ahead on the left is the paddock Trent told him about. Just off the main road. A site once used for training greyhounds. Vacant now for more than a decade but the track still exists. Bitchin' for doin' a few laps, or so Trent has told him.

He pushes the Lexus up to eighty, ninety, one hundred. Thirty kilometres over the posted limit; ten above the legal limit for his provisional licence. One hundred and ten and it barely feels like he's moving, the ride is that smooth. The bushland lining the roadway seems to fly past. The white centreline is a path laid out just for him, like the driving line in a video game. He imagines he can see spectators standing along the roadside, cheering him on to even greater speeds. They wave their arms and clap and cheer and he steers the Lexus until it straddles the line. Around a slow right-hander, tyres squealing. One-twenty. One-thirty. And the blazing headlights of an oncoming vehicle draw a sheet of white across his vision. The long blare of a horn.

Ryan jerks the wheel left. Blinks. Blinks again. Feels the car begin to slide and tries to correct. Was it turn into or turn out of a slide? He doesn't remember. Doesn't have time to think. Just turns the wheel hard-lock to the right and jams his foot on the brake. His vision clears in time to see a truck barrelling past, mere centimetres from the side window, and the Lexus slews in behind it. He catches a glimpse of red, the truck's tail-lights receding into the distance, and the car continues its spin until he's facing back the way he was originally travelling. Only now, he's on the wrong side of the road.

He taps gently on the accelerator. Turns the car and steers back to the right side of the road. Stops on the verge. His heart is thumping in his chest. Mouth dry and his breathing like the panting of a dog. It hurts to peel his white-knuckled fingers from the steering wheel and the music is still pounding, pounding in his ears and through the chassis of the car. He feels terrified and excited and so very, very alive.

He switches the stereo off and stares out through the windscreen. The spectators he'd imagined standing by the roadside are still there, but no longer clapping or cheering. In the glow of his headlights their pale faces appear disappointed, disgusted even, with his performance. You lost it, bud, their eyes seem to say. You could have gone faster. You could have really torn this road up like it was your own. He feels that disappointment too, deep down inside, as the flood of adrenalin dissipates and leaves his body shaking. Only one hundred and thirty, he thinks, and I couldn't even handle that. So much for a top speed of two fifty. What would Trent think of the useless city kid now?

He sees Grant, standing amongst the spectators, eyes still bruised and puffed up to tight little slits. Grant is smiling and Ryan can see half his teeth are missing, others jagged where they've been snapped off. Blood runs down his chin from the split in his lip. The bandage on his head is gone and a long flap of raw, red skin hangs from his skull and over his left ear. He's shaking his head and the flap of skin flutters with each movement. His hand comes up, fingers clenched except for the pinky which dangles at an obscene angle, and he gives Ryan a big thumbs down.

Ryan reaches out, trembling all over, and switches off the headlights. Grant and the other spectators disappear, like they were nothing but projections. He wonders for a moment if they were ever there. All that is left to see are the dark shapes of trees and the white crosses that adorn their trunks.

"Sup bro? You're late. You okay? You look like you seen a ghost."

Ryan isn't sure if Trent's smile is a sly and knowing one, or if he's just excited at the sight of the Lexus. Down on the track a Ford and a Holden are revving the guts out of their engines, ready to prove once and for all which is the superior vehicle.

"This your dad's car, huh? Nice. Can't wait to see how it handles. V6, yeah?"

"Yeah."

Ryan isn't sure about taking it for a spin on the track. It looks kind of dusty. His dad will kill him if he turns up at the hospital with it covered in dirt. That will only mean a barrage of questions he can't answer truthfully. He's supposed to be at a games night. And there's the still fresh memory of what happened out on the road. He'd thought about turning around and heading straight home but the worry of what Trent, Boof and Stevo would think if he bailed had trumped his fears again.

"What'd it cost? Forty? Fifty grand?"

"Closer to ninety when he bought it, I think?"

"Fuck me! That's some serious money, bro. What's your old man doin' out here in the boonies?"

"That's what my mum wants to know. Mid-life crisis? Says he's fed up giving botox injections to stuck up cougars with chihuahuas and diamond studded handbags. Wants to do some good for a change."

"Ha! Out here? That's a laugh. I'd be stickin' it to those bitches day and night. Come on, let's go watch the race."

Boof and Stevo are waiting at the edge of the track as the Ford and the Holden shift into gear and take off. The cars spew up dust and the boys are cheering. There are perhaps twenty or thirty others standing around. Not all are teenage boys. There are some older guys, maybe early twenties, and a few girls too. Everyone's hooting and hollering above the sound of the engines.

"Hey? You hear about Grant?" Stevo asks.

Ryan nods but says nothing about him being there in

the hospital when Grant died. Nothing about Grant's last words, and definitely nothing about seeing him out on Bundarra Road.

"We've put you down for the next run. Up against a WRX. Think you'll be able to take it?" Boof points of towards a silver Subaru.

"What's the driver like? Any good?"

"Fuck no! He's a pussy. And the WRX is just stock."

"Shouldn't be a problem then."

The Ford and the Holden round the final curve of the track. The Holden is drifting sideways around the corner and its back-end clips the front-right corner of the Ford with a crunch. Glass flies from the impact, littering the track like diamonds and rubies. Ryan winces and thinks of the Lexus with a smashed headlight. The Holden straightens up on the final run to the finish line but the Ford has already passed on the inside and pulled ahead. The last fifty metres are a forgone conclusion and already there are shouts of victory and abuse. Ryan sees money changing hands amongst the crowd.

"People bet on this?"

"Yeah, 'course they do." Trent's smiling. "I've already put fifty bucks on you."

A girl stands by the side of the track wearing nothing but jeans and a black, lace bra. She holds her shirt high above her head as Ryan revs the engine of the Lexus. He's seen her at school. A gorgeous Year 12 student with long dark hair and milky skin. Way out of his league. Rumour is she's screwing her Math teacher.

Ryan risks a quick glance across at the WRX. Some guy he's never seen before is behind the wheel. Must be twenty-five, at least. Ryan knows the WRX will have the jump on him. It's a manual and the Lexus is a semi-automatic, but he has no idea how to shift it into manual mode. He's guessing he won't be behind for very long though. All he needs to do is make sure he stays on the track and out of the Subaru's way. That's the only bit he's really worried about. Staying on the track. He's never driven on dirt before.

The girl brings her shirt down in a long graceful sweep and Ryan is caught off guard. The WRX pulls away, leaving him sitting in a cloud of dust. He can see people standing on the sidelines; some cheering the WRX, some laughing at him. He hits the accelerator and the wheels spin until they gain traction. Then the Lexus is moving forward. It cuts through the dust cloud, parting it, and Ryan can see the WRX about twenty metres ahead. By the time the Subaru swings into the first left-hand bend, he is only a car length behind. He pulls wide, hoping to overtake on the outside but the guy must have caught sight of him in his rear-view mirror because the Subaru is pulling across to block his path. He eases off on the accelerator to prevent spinning out and turns the Lexus down into the curve. Accelerates hard as soon as he's found a good line. Passes the WRX on the inside.

Didn't see that coming did you? Ryan thinks. He can see spectators standing by the side of the track. There seems to be more of them now. Fifty or sixty. They're jumping up and down, waving shirts and cans of beer. He wonders where they've all come from. Strange that he can even hear them over the sound of the engine, but he can. Like a stadium crowd, and they're all cheering for him.

He comes out of the first bend doing almost one-twenty. The back-end fishtails a little but he's waiting for that and corrects by gently counter steering. In his rear-view mirror he can see the WRX a few car lengths behind. It has taken the turn better than the Lexus, drifting through the corner so it's already lined up when it hits the straight. Hard to believe, but it is catching up and Ryan realises he's being much too cautious.

"Come on, man," a voice says beside him. "You can take this sucker."

Ryan looks across to the empty passenger seat, taking his eyes off the track for an instant. The seat is no longer empty. Grant sits there. He's smiling at Ryan, blood dry and black on his chin.

"Geez, Ryan! You know how fast this thing can go," Grant lisps through shattered teeth. "Give it some juice. Trent's got money on you, man! He'll be pissed if he loses it. You want the boys to see what a pussy you are?"

Ryan doesn't want that, no way. He wants to show them that he's as good as any of them. Better even. He pushes down on the accelerator and the speedometer moves up to one-thirty, one-forty, one-fifty. He's not sure what the WRX's top speed is but finally it's falling behind. He steers the Lexus wide on the long, final curve. Eases off the accelerator a fraction and turns down into the corner. Floors it again coming out of the curve and he's back onto the final straight, still doing one hundred and fifty kilometres an hour. The crowd is going wild.

"That's the way, bro! Now give 'em something to really fuckin' cheer about."

Ryan doesn't believe that Grant is really sitting beside him. It is just some figment of his imagination. Stress from what he saw at the hospital. He's never been so close to death before and he knows psychological side-effects are inevitable. But would they seem so real? And what about all the people cheering him on? So many, and half of them so pale faced and sunken eyed. He can still hear them, their adulation filling him with pride, fuelling his excitement and the adrenalin rush that's pushing him to push the car. One-sixty. One-seventy. One-eighty across the finish line. He's at least three car lengths ahead and he begins to laugh. Grant joins in, a wet sound that gurgles up from deep within his throat.

Only then does Ryan realise how fast he's going and how little straight track remains ahead. It is a reflex for him to slam on the brakes. The car's nose dips. Dirt sprays up over the bonnet, coating the windscreen in dust. Ryan turns the wheel hard-left and Grant is still laughing as the car begins to slide. Turns side on. Continues around in a one-eighty degree spin until the car stops, facing back along the track towards the finish line.

The laughter stops too and Ryan realises he is sitting alone. His heart beats like a motherfucker and he's filled with a euphoria of achievement. A feeling of having accomplished something wonderful and dangerous and survived to enjoy it.

He reaches out and turns on the windscreen wipers. The blades scrape away dust in two great arcs until his view is clear again. Trent and Stevo and Boof have already jumped the railing and are on their way over. Trent is waving a handful of cash. Beyond the rail he can see the rest of the crowd. Some have gone back to talking amongst themselves. A small number continue to look his way, clapping and pointing. But there are others too, that large number of people he didn't see until after he'd started racing, and they appear different from the rest.

Insubstantial, like reflections on the windscreen, fading slowly into nothingness. They are all — these figments, these ghosts — staring directly at him, staring *into* him, and they don't look happy with his performance at all.

"You look like somethin's botherin' you, bro. Worried that I ended up with all the cash? Should'a placed a bet on yourself."

They're walking back to their cars after watching the last couple of races. One guy blew the engine of his Toyota twin-cab on the starting line and some out-of-towner put his Nissan through the rail on the first turn. Otherwise, it was a quiet night according to Trent.

"Nah, it's not that," Ryan says. "It's all that dust. Dad's gonna be pissed."

This is true, but it isn't what's bothering him. It's the thought that he could have done better off the line. That he should have taken that first corner a lot cleaner than he did. Maybe then he could have picked up some more speed. Maybe pushed the Lexus up closer to that 250 km/h. And he's a little bothered that this is bothering him. It isn't like him at all. Closest he's ever been to something like this is a few laps on Forza or Gran Tourismo on the Xbox. He never would have dreamed of driving that fast in the city. But he can't deny that it felt good.

"Nah, don't worry 'bout it. There's a late night servo in town. They've got a car wash. Your old man won't notice a thing."

"You ever race out there yourself?"

"Yeah, course. Best feeling in the world, man. Just you

and the car and everyone outside cheerin' you on."

"You ever seen anyone else out there trackside? People you don't know? People you used to know?"

"Always people here I don't know. People from other towns lookin' to try their luck against the locals."

Ryan shakes his head. He doesn't know how to say what he wants to say.

"Nah, not what I meant. Doesn't matter. Not important anyway. Look, I gotta go. Have to pick my dad up at eleven and I've gotta get the car cleaned up first."

"Sure thing, bro. You did pretty well for a first timer."

They shake hands and Trent palms a couple of twenty dollar bills across.

"Your share. Place a bet on yourself next time. You're a natural. Grant woulda been proud."

Before Ryan can say anything, Trent turns and walks away.

Ryan drives out of the old greyhound track and onto Bundarra Road. He heads back towards town, driving cautiously and right on the speed limit. All the while he's thinking about the pale faces in the crowd. About Grant and what he said in his final moments at the hospital. The people standing mute beside their crosses. He finds it strange that he's not scared by any of this. Instead, he feels excited by their presence. Daring. Fearless. Someone he'd never normally be.

It is not quite ten-thirty. Still time to get the car cleaned up and make it to the hospital before eleven. He drives in silence, preferring it for the moment to the thump, thump,

thump of bass beats. His window is wound down and through it he can hear the gentle purr of the engine. Cicadas and crickets and the sound of the wind rushing by.

The harsh blue-white of halogen headlamps flare in the rear-view mirror, throwing his shadow across the instrument panel. He looks up and sees a car coming up behind. He doesn't speed up or pull over. Just continues driving the way he has been. He's on a nice long straight. The way is clear and there is plenty of room for the other car to pass. It comes up close behind the Lexus anyway, close enough that Ryan can no longer see its lights. The car blares its horn and Ryan is tempted to tap his brakes. See if the guy will back off. As soon as he thinks this the car pulls out on to the other side of the road. Brings itself up level with the Lexus.

It's the guy in the WRX. He's looking across at Ryan and smiling. Revving the WRX so that it surges forward then drops back level again. It's all a taunt.

"Go on, show him who's boss, Ryan."

The voice comes from the back-seat and Ryan looks up into the rear-view mirror. The boy sitting there, Ryan has only seen his face once. In a single school photograph nailed to a tree. His eye sockets are dark and hollow, face drained of colour, but Ryan is sure it is Pete. One of his collar bones, white and snapped off at the end, juts from a wound just below his neck.

"Yeah, man. Pete's right. Show him you're the shiz."

Grant is back in the passenger seat, nodding and agreeing. The flap of skin hanging from his skull wobbles like an emo's comb-over.

"What can this thing do?" Pete asks. "Two hundred? Two fifty? That arsehole in his jap crap probably can't even do half that."

"Yeah, we've seen how you drive. You're a master, man. The best this town has seen. Don't wanna let a shithead like that think otherwise."

And they're right. Just because he's the new kid from the city doesn't mean he can let others think he's a pushover. He's got to prove himself. Not just to the dickhead in the WRX, but to himself as well. He accelerates and edges the Lexus forward just a little. The WRX follows suit and they're neck and neck again. Ryan smiles across at the driver. Gives the guy the middle finger and speeds up. The speedometer is already touching one hundred and twenty.

The WRX drops back a car length and Ryan smiles. Too easy, he thinks, and then the WRX growls. It shoots forward, level with the Lexus for a moment. Ryan hears the turbocharger kick in and the WRX roars ahead. It is two car lengths in front and pulling back onto Ryan's side of the road before he can react. He pushes his foot to the floor and the Lexus takes off. One-thirty. One-forty. One-fifty. Grant and Pete are whooping with delight as Ryan brings the Lexus to within a metre of the WRX's rear bumper. Steers right, onto the wrong side of the road. Hits the accelerator and brings himself back level with the WRX. He smiles at the driver. Waves bye-bye and pushes the Lexus as hard as he can.

"That's the way, Ryan. Now you're teachin' that fucker a lesson," Grant crows. Pete is laughing and slapping the back of Ryan's seat. The Lexus is overtaking but the other driver is pushing the WRX too. One-sixty. One-seventy. One-eighty. The WRX is only half a car-length behind. Pete winds down the passenger window, sticks his arse out and moons the other driver. Ryan is sure the driver can't see any of that. His passengers are all in his imagination, not a shared illusion. Why then can he feel the wind blowing harder than it was before?

The speedometer hits two hundred kilometres an hour and still the Lexus is barely in the lead. Certainly not far enough ahead for Ryan to steer back onto the right side of the road without clipping the WRX's front-end. He knows the end of the straight is coming up soon. But in the onrushing darkness and the bare few metres illuminated by the car's headlights, he has no idea where the next bend is.

"Go, go, go, go!" Pete and Grant are chanting. Red spittle from Grant's lip spatters the inside of the windscreen. I'll have to clean that too, Ryan thinks an instant before he realises it's not real. None of it is real. There is nobody here in the car with him because there can't be. Pete and Grant are dead. He sat in Pete's twisted wreckage of a car. Saw Grant go into convulsions on a hospital bed. He's alone, on the wrong side of the road, doing just under two hundred and twenty kilometres an hour.

He looks across and the passenger seat is empty. Through the side window he sees the WRX drop away, hears it working down through gears. He looks up into the rear-view mirror, no Pete. The Subaru is falling way behind. The red of its brake lights reflect off the road's surface. He feels a moment of jubilation — that he's won, the guy has given up — and returns his eyes to the road ahead.

A white guard rail marks the end of the straight, a sharp left turn disappearing into darkness. Ryan spins the wheel and slams on the brakes but it is too late. The Lexus hits the guard rail at an angle. Goes straight over the top. For a few metres the car is airborne, sailing through the night and a cool wind blowing through the open window. The air-bags deploy with a sound like a gunshot. White dust fills the cabin an instant before the driver's side bag smashes into Ryan's face, shattering his nose. At the speed the Lexus is travelling, even this modern safety feature is largely ineffectual. The car hits a tree at a point almost two metres above the ground, still moving at close to two hundred kilometres an hour.

The driver's side door crumples around the age hardened trunk of the eucalypt. Ryan is slammed sideways. His seatbelt locks, holding his body in place but his head and neck continue on, wrenching muscles from their connective tissue. The jagged end of a branch penetrates the floor, the car seat, Ryan's thigh. He can't feel anything down the right side of his body. His arms flop like things made of rubber, too many bends for just elbow and wrist. Glass is shattering all around, tiny pieces floating in the air like stars. His head whips back towards the open window and collides with the tree. He hears something crack and tear and warm blood flows down the side of his face. He turns to look at the tree as the car begins to fall, everything moving so slowly, and sees his ear caught between two pieces of bark. It seems even less real than Grant and Pete cheering him on.

As the Lexus hits the ground and bounces and rolls he's thinking, I never apologised to mum. I never got to tell her I was sorry.

Out on Bundarra Road, Ryan gulps greedily at the beer Trent has poured. He sucks it from the earth and pulls at

243

the cigarette that has been stuck in the dirt. Stevo and Boof are there. So are a few kids he doesn't know. Kids from school he never met. But they're here now, sitting before his white cross, talking about him in tones of reverence and awe. He hates them all.

The cross is his mother's work. A simple object of painted plywood nailed directly into the tree's trunk. She promises it is only temporary. That she'll make him a better one. Bouquets of fresh flowers have been arranged around the base of the tree, jostling for position with a growing pile of beer cans that his mother is forever trying to clear away. There is a photograph too. One where he's standing on a stage at his old school, accepting an award for academic excellence. He looks like a nerd. It's a photograph that his father took. A snapshot of a moment his parents were both so proud of.

His father has never been to visit. Probably never will. He was waiting at the hospital for Ryan to pick him up when the ambulance pulled in. His father the first to rush over and offer assistance. The first to pull back the sheet on the gurney. It was his job and it had never been easy, but Ryan is certain his father never expected to see his own son that way. No, his father will not visit. Not ever.

His mum still comes though. Fresh flowers every week and always a new apology that isn't owed. She never blames him. She blames the cars and the roads. She blames herself, and her husband. Mostly, she blames the boys who come here to drink with him. Ryan blames them too. For the life they can look forward to, the life he's lost, and for that he wishes they were here with him too.

He has Pete and Grant and all the others though. They stand by their crosses, unseen by those who hero worship them. But essentially, they are alone. Waiting for visitors to come. For another race day or for a car to drive too fast on the road so they too can join in the fun. The thrill of the ride.

Trent is telling another bullshit anecdote. The boys are all clustered around him, drunk and enraptured by his tale. Out on the road, a car is coming along, headlights cutting through the night.

Ryan steps away from the morbid congregation of teenagers. Walks to the road's rough gravel verge. The others are already there, lined up for a mile in either direction, waiting for the car to arrive. They all cheer as it nears, egging it on. Ryan shouts with them. Faster, faster you bastard! Come on, you can do it. And somehow, the driver picks up on this. As it passes, the car accelerates to well over the legal limit and goes screeching around a bend.

**Mike Brooks** lives in Nottingham, England, with his wife, cats and an ever-changing number of tropical fish. He works in a homeless hostel and spends his spare time writing fiction, playing in a couple of bands and DJing wherever anyone will tolerate him.

Henri René Albert **Guy de Maupassant** (5 August 1850– 6 July 1893) was a popular 19th-century French writer, considered one of the fathers of the modern short story and one of the form's finest exponents. He authored some 300 short stories, six novels, three travel books, and one volume of verse. (Bio courtesy of wikipedia.com.)

**Chris Donahue** is an electrical engineer, former Navy avionics tech, brewer, history buff, wargamer and writer living in the Dallas area. He shares his life with his wife (and fellow author), Linda, and an assortment of deadbeat critters.

**Robert Essig** lives in the southwestern most corner of the United States with his wife, son, and dog. He writes frightening tales and has published over 30 short stories, two novellas, and one novel. Visit him on the web at robertessig.blogspot.com.

The fiction of **Lindsey Goddard** has been sprinkling the horror genre since her first small-press publication at the age of fifteen. Her stories have been published in numerous magazines and in the anthologies: Ladies of Horror, From the Mouth, End of Days 2, It Was a Dark and Stormy Halloween, and Forrest J. Ackerman's The Anthology of the Living Dead. Her poetry has appeared in Niteblade and Black Petals and in the print anthology Scattered Verses Moonlit Curses. She resides in the suburbs of St. Louis, MO with her husband, three children and a daft feline companion. Visit her at www.lindseybethgoddard.com

**Carole Hall** is a native of the UK, now living in California. She has 53 short stories published and a novel on e-books called *Killing at the White Swan Inn*. She lives with her best friend, a massage therapist, and two Siamese cats. She began reading at five years of age when her mother refused to read the end of fairy tales, telling her, "You have to find out for yourself", so she did. She is currently awaiting a publisher for her second novel: *Nairobi Bloodstar*.

**JC Hemphill** was born yesterday, so if you find his writing infantile ... you're spot-on. But you gotta admit, he's pretty damn good for a toddler. Winner of *The Washington Pastime Literary Contest*, his work has appeared in *Pulp Modern, Dark Tales of Lost Civilizations, SNM Horror Magazine, Bonded by Blood 4: Best of 2011, Spinetinglers, Stories in the Ether, & ShadowCast Audio* with upcoming work in *Buzzy Mag, Bloodtide, & Cover of Darkness*. Follow his scribblings on Facebook or at www.jchemphill.com/

**Tim Jeffreys** is the author of three collections of short stories, *The Garden Where Black Flowers Grow*, *The Scenery of Dreams*, and *The Haunted Grove*, as well as the first book of his Thief saga: *Thief's Return.*

The majority of his stories are hard to pigeonhole, and are best described as a mix of horror, fairytale, black comedy, and everyday life. He is also a talented artist and illustrates some of his books with his own drawings.

Originally from Manchester, England, Tim now lives in Bristol where he is kept sane by his partner, Isabel, and his lovely baby daughter. Visit him at his website, found at www.timjeffreyswriter.webs.com.

**C. I. Kemp** is the pen name of a member of the Northern New Jersey Grotto, an organization dedicated to cave preservation. He has had numerous articles published in that organization's newsletter and participated in cave rescue simulations. His caving experience was the subject of an article in the June 2006 issue of 201, a magazine dedicated to activities in Bergen County, New Jersey. The descriptions and non-supernatural events in the story are drawn from his personal experience.

**Lisamarie Lamb** was five when she wrote her first short story - it involved a car going over a cliff, Jessica Fletcher and the Phantom Raspberry Blower. It didn't have much of a plot but it did make her realise that writing was for her.

Over the years she has written various short stories, plays, poems and novels in different genres, including romance and children's books. She has a blog in which she showcases flash fiction, themoonlitdoor.blogspot.com.

She has self-published a horror novel, *Mother's Helper*, and a collection of short stories entitled *Some Body's at the Door*. She is also part of four published anthologies and has been accepted into eight more.

**Andrew J McKiernan** is an author and illustrator living and working on the Central Coast of NSW. First published in 2007, his stories and illustrations have since been nominated for multiple Aurealis, Ditmar and Australian Shadows awards. His work can be found appearing here and there, like a slow growing fungus.

**Robert J. Mendenhall** is a retired police officer and currently serves on active duty with the Wisconsin Air National Guard. An active member of Science Fiction and Fantasy Writers of America, his short fiction has appeared in three Star Trek Strange New Worlds anthologies published by Pocket Books. He has also been published in Crimespree Magazine, The Martian Wave, and Cosmic Crime Stories, and has works soon to be published in Aoife's Kiss Magazine and Alternative Witness Magazine. Internet appearances include WanderingsMag.com, Mindflights.com, and ResAliens.com. He lives outside Chicago with his wife and fellow writer, Claire, and many animals.

This is **Stephen Patrick**'s third incarnation as a writer. As a young boy, he wrote what his teachers told him, simple tales about the things around him. As a young man, he wrote for school or for work, or sometimes just to get the story out of his thoughts and onto the page. Now, he lets his imagination guide him to wherever a story needs to go.

    He has written short stories in genres from sci fi/fantasy to historical to horror. His newest passion is film racing, including four short films as writer with Elephant and Castle Productions.

**Edgar Allan Poe** (19 January 1809–7 October 1849) was an American author, poet, editor and literary critic, considered part of the American Romantic Movement.

Best known for his tales of mystery and the macabre, Poe was one of the earliest American practitioners of the short story and is considered the inventor of the detective fiction genre. He is further credited with contributing to the emerging genre of science fiction. (Bio courtesy of wikipedia.com.)

Fort Worth writer **Jonathan Shipley** has had fantasy, science fiction, and horror stories published in magazines and a dozen plus anthologies. However, he is actually a novel writer at heart and spends most of his writing time on a vast story arc that ranges from Nazi occultism to vampires to futuristic space opera. A complete list of published stories may be found on Wikipedia (search Jonathan Shipley the writer, not the dead bishop) and on his website at www.shipleyscifi.com.

Samuel Langhorne Clemens (30 November 1835–21 April 1910), better known by his pen name **Mark Twain**, was an American author and humorist. He is most noted for his novels, *The Adventures of Tom Sawyer* (1876), and its sequel, *Adventures of Huckleberry Finn* (1885), the latter often called "the Great American Novel". (Bio courtesy of wikipedia.com.)

When not writing or working as a wildlife biologist, **Sabrina West** roams the streets of San Diego. There, she hunts rare songbirds, quality espresso, and elusive snippets of dialogue and imagery. Her short fiction has appeared in markets such as the Santa Clara Review, Cover of Darkness, and Strange, Weird and Wonderful Magazine. Sabrina blogs about writing and life at theprosers.blogspot.com.

# Tomorrow

## Post-Apocolyptic Short Stories

None of us know what will happen tomorrow. The world, as we know it, could change overnight. Will there be famine, plague, or aliens? Will we advance in technology or go back to feudalistic ways? Will we have to travel the universe to find a new planet, a new home? The *Tomorrow* anthology will explore the possibilities.

The speculative fiction stories in this book will be full of action and excitement, uncertainty and fear, struggles, destruction and mayhem.

**Due for release in paperback and various digital formats in late 2012.**

Check our website for updates:
http://www.kayellepress.com

CPSIA information can be obtained at www.ICGtesting.com
Printed in the USA
BVOW061021290512

291297BV00004B/18/P